Southern Charm
& Second Chances

Nancy Robards Thompson

HARLEQUIN
SPECIAL
EDITION

ISBN-13: 978-1-335-89451-9

Southern Charm & Second Chances

Copyright © 2020 by Nancy Robards Thompson

This edition published by arrangement with Harlequin Books S.A.

For questions and comments about the quality of this book,
please contact us at CustomerService@Harlequin.com.

Harlequin Enterprises ULC
22 Adelaide St. West, 40th Floor
Toronto, Ontario M5H 4E3, Canada
www.Harlequin.com

Printed in U.S.A.

Dear Reader,

When I'm not writing, I love to cook and bake. I came about it naturally because my family has always been all about food. Every celebration was centered around food, and when extended family is together, often we can't leave one meal without starting to talk about the next. That's because, to us, food symbolizes love.

I had such fun when it came to writing Jane and Liam's story. It's set in a restaurant in Savannah and features Jane's big femalecentric family. Through Jane and her family, Liam learns how to love and forgive.

I hope you enjoy the story as much as I loved writing it. Please drop me a line and let me know— Nancy@NancyRobardsThompson.com.

Warmly,

Nancy

Liam peered into the bowl. "What are you working on?"

"A new savory bread recipe I came up with."

"Tell me about it."

"It's a beer bread with a blend of herbs and cheese that I'm in the process of perfecting."

"That's why I smell beer. I thought maybe I'd driven you to drink."

He said the words with a straight face, but Jane gathered this was his attempt at showing that he had a sense of humor.

Two could play that game.

"Apparently you have." She picked up the bottle, held it up to him in a toast and sipped.

"Mind if I join you?" he said.

"That means you're staying awhile?" she asked.

"Unless I'm intruding."

"Of course not. It's your place." She motioned for him to follow her. "Come with me and I'll show you Charles's food-and-beverage sign-out system."

At the pantry, he stopped at the door and, with one hand holding it open, he motioned for her to go first. If she hadn't been distracted by his good manners, she would've remind him to make sure the doorstop was in place so the door didn't—

The door slammed shut.

THE SAVANNAH SISTERS: One historic inn, two meddling matchmakers, three Savannah sisters.

National bestselling author **Nancy Robards Thompson** holds a degree in journalism. She worked as a newspaper reporter until she realized reporting "just the facts" bored her silly. Now that she has much more content to report to her muse, Nancy loves writing women's fiction and romance full-time. Critics have deemed her work "funny, smart and observant." She resides in Florida with her husband and daughter. You can reach her at Facebook.com/nrobardsthompson.

Books by Nancy Robards Thompson

Harlequin Special Edition

The Savannah Sisters

A Down-Home Savannah Christmas

Celebration, TX

The Cowboy's Runaway Bride
A Bride, a Barn, and a Baby
The Cowboy Who Got Away

The Fortunes of Texas: The Lost Fortunes

A Fortunate Arrangement

The Fortunes of Texas: Rulebreakers

Maddie Fortune's Perfect Man

The Fortunes of Texas: The Secret Fortunes

Fortune's Surprise Engagement

Visit the Author Profile page
at Harlequin.com for more titles.

This book is dedicated to Gail Chasan for bringing me into the Harlequin family all those years ago. Thanks for everything!

Chapter One

Jane Clark was having a nightmare.

Why else would Liam Wright be standing in front of her—in Savannah—in the middle of the restaurant that had become her sanctuary, eight hundred miles from the humiliation and bad memories born of the last time they'd spoken?

The restaurant opened at five o'clock, but Charles Weathersby, owner of Wila, had summoned the entire staff—both front-of-the-house and kitchen—for an early morning meeting. Why, then, was Chef Liam Wright here, darkening the Wila dining room with his perpetual scowl?

Jane fisted her hands and felt the bite of nails digging into flesh.

Nope. It wasn't a nightmare. She was wide awake.

God!

If this wasn't a bad dream, it had to be a cruel joke. Because that was the only other explanation for his being in Savannah instead of terrorizing his own minions at La Bula, his New York City restaurant.

Jane glanced around the dining room. Its black-and-white marble floors and polished dark wood contrasted with the light airiness of the glass from the windows and mirrors, which reflected the crystal chandeliers and pops of color from the red banquettes lining the back wall. It was so early, the front-house staff hadn't had a chance to set the tables for that evening's dinner. Soon they would cover the tables with crisp white cloths and napkins, and adorn the tops with a single red rose in a bud vase. A single red rose had become synonymous with Wila, its image on the cover of the menus and used in all of their advertising.

The familiarity of Wila was comforting to Jane. It was a touchstone that reminded her that she was safe here. She had done well here. She wasn't defined by past missteps.

Judging from the way her coworkers murmured among themselves as they sat in the empty dining room waiting for the meeting to start, she wasn't the only one wondering why Liam was there.

Charles clapped his hands. "Boys and girls," he said, his Southern gentleman's drawl elongating the words. "May I have your attention, please?"

When everyone quieted down, he continued. "Thank y'all for obliging me and coming in early on such short notice. I'm sure all y'all know Liam Wright. He's the owner and executive chef of La Bula in New York City, as well as a winner of the prestigious Oscar Hurd Foundation Award and a past champion of the renowned television cooking show, *America's Best Chef.*"

Liam seemed to bask in the glory of his résumé as he looked everywhere except at Jane. She couldn't decide if that was a good thing—maybe he didn't recognize her. Was it possible he didn't remember her? Yeah—*no*. Fat chance. More like he was purposely avoiding eye contact after the way he'd treated her the last time they'd seen each other.

Pinpricks of shame needled Jane. Until now, she had managed to shelve the humiliation as she'd made an earnest attempt to move on with her life. And she had been getting on beautifully. Charles was happy with her work. Just a few nights ago, he'd confirmed that Wila's revenues from dessert sales had never been higher. She'd even managed to score a feature in the *Savannah Morning News*. The food editor had interviewed her and sent a photographer who'd made the array of desserts Jane had prepared for the occasion look like works of art. She couldn't have paid for better PR for herself and for the restaurant.

Things were going so well.

She took a deep breath and filled her lungs with air, pushing past the tentacles of dread that had wrapped themselves around her windpipe, intent on suffocating her. She needed to stop overthinking things.

Look how far you've come. Focus on that.

Charles was an old family friend. She'd worked for him at Wila when she'd been in high school. He'd hired her again without question when she'd returned to Savannah. He hadn't asked for specifics about why she'd left her job in New York and she hadn't supplied them.

It had been that cut and dried, and everything had been working out fine.

Of course, it was entirely possible that Liam hadn't showed up to ruin her life—again. Maybe he was in town and he'd popped in to see Charles, one professional to another. Maybe he'd even have dinner at Wila tonight. If he did, it could be a good opportunity. Jane would serve him rum baba. The ironic gesture would fulfill two purposes. One, it would show him that his visit didn't fluster her one bit. And two, it would prove that she really did know what she was doing. In fact, she'd make sure the cake was so delicious it would knock his socks off. It would break the ice and they would have a good laugh over the rum baba debacle that had made him lose it and send her packing last year.

"Many of you know that I've been eyeing retirement," Charles said, interrupting the reunion scene playing in Jane's head. "Even though this old body is tired and ready for a long vacation, I've decided it's not time for me to completely bow out. Not just yet. However, I am ready to lighten my load a bit. That's why I've decided to bring on a partner."

A partner?

A couple of choice words went through Jane's head as her stomach dropped to somewhere around her ankles.

Oh, dear God, no. Not Liam Wright. Please.

Even though she knew what Charles was going to say before he said it, she still wasn't ready for the blow.

"I didn't want to bring just anyone on board. I need someone creative, someone with a keen understanding of fine dining and a flare for approachable luxury. At the same time, I realized it might be a good time to make some changes that will make Wila more competitive and cutting edge without losing the clientele and the timeless feel I've worked my entire life to cultivate… Liam Wright is a natural fit. So, effective immediately, Chef Wright and I will be partners and he will help us begin the transition into our new phase.

"He will be here for the next month, working with you to refine the menu and implement the changes we need to make to achieve our new vision. Just so you know, we will be closed for a week, beginning Sunday, so that he can bring you up to speed on the new practices and procedures. But I will let him tell you more about our new and improved vision for Wila. Please join me in welcoming Chef Wright to Savannah."

Charles started the clapping. Jane joined in because it would've been rude not to, and it was the best way to show Liam that she was doing fine. Perfectly fine. But that didn't stop her extremities from going numb as she watched Liam exchange a few quiet words with Charles before he addressed the staff.

"What the hell?" murmured Joe Donoghue, Wila's sous chef. "Have you heard anything about this?"

Not wanting to discuss it, Jane answered with a quick shake of her head. Joe cursed under his breath, finally settling on one choice word that he muttered over and over under his breath like a banishing spell.

"Thanks, everyone," Liam finally said. He was dressed in jeans and a black Henley shirt that hugged his broad shoulders and solid chest. Her favorite body type on a guy—toned, but carrying enough meat that proved he was healthy, that he was not a slave to diets and the gym. He was tall—in the six-two, six-three range, she guessed—with dark hair and dark, dark eyes. No matter how Jane felt about him, there was no denying the sum of the parts added up to one very good-looking guy.

He knew it, too.

He was infamous for dating models. And he carried himself in a smug, too-cool-for-school, *I'm sexy and I know it* way that had always irked her. It still did.

Charles's phone rang. He looked at the screen. "I need to take this call. Everyone, make Liam feel welcome." With the phone pressed to his ear, Charles disappeared into the kitchen.

"It's good to be here," Liam said. "Savannah is one of my favorite places in the world. That's why I was stoked when Charles approached me about joining the team here at Wila. And that's what we will be—*a team*."

He paused, unsmiling, and glanced around the room as if driving home the point. His gaze landed on Jane.

"I already know at least one of you."

Oh, great. Oh, God.

Her mouth went dry and her heart folded in on itself. The look on Liam's face wasn't damning, but it didn't exactly fill her with the warm fuzzy feeling of opportunity, either. Jane managed to lift the corners of her mouth into what she hoped was a convincing smile, one she would share with an acquaintance.

No need to antagonize the beast.

Especially when he would be her boss.

Again.

She hoped.

Because the alternative would mean more professional upheaval, and she'd just gotten settled.

"If you would," Liam said, "let's go around the room and each of you introduce yourself and tell me what you do around here. Let's start with Jane over there."

He remembered her name.

The tentacles of dread tightened and Jane suddenly found it hard to catch her breath. Because… well, she hadn't exactly lied to Charles. *No*, she hadn't lied at all. She just hadn't told him why she'd retuned to Savannah and needed a job after going to culinary school and working in one of the hottest restaurants in New York City.

She hadn't volunteered the reason behind her homecoming. It had been too humiliating. She had made such a stupid mistake and, in the end, she'd let herself down, which had almost hurt more than being fired by "America's Best Chef."

Almost.

After the dust had settled, she'd had a hard time finding another job in New York as an executive pastry chef at the level at which she'd been working. Jobs just weren't that plentiful. Finally, when Charles had made her the offer, she'd had no choice but to come back to Savannah.

While she'd been grateful for the job, she hadn't been very excited about coming home. Savannah was a far cry from New York.

In many ways, she'd been just as snobby and too sophisticated as she'd mentally accused Liam of being.

But her case was totally different.

Even so, she'd suffered because of the firing.

She'd just gotten her mojo back. Things were just starting to happen for her. She'd missed Savannah more than she realized. She was feeling at home here. In fact, she'd recently turned down two job offers—one in Hilton Head and one in Atlanta—because this job felt right. Charles gave her the freedom to experiment and try new things. It was amazing the things she could accomplish when she didn't have to fear making a mistake, which is what she'd lived with every day at La Bula.

Now, she'd come to work this morning only to find the big, bad wolf huffing and puffing and threatening to blow down the life she'd rebuilt. But first, Liam wanted her to reintroduce herself to him. In front of everyone.

The last time she'd seen him, he'd embarrassed her in front of her La Bula coworkers. Every single word he'd said had been true. But what had hurt almost as badly as making the mistake was the way he'd called her out in front of everyone—his temper going from subzero to blazing in a matter of seconds.

Though she'd done nothing wrong, she was at his mercy again.

The best way to deal with Liam Wright was to hold her head high and look him in the eyes.

She swallowed and composed her expression so that her face wouldn't betray how utterly nauseated she felt.

"Welcome, chef. As you know, I'm Jane Clark. Previously, I worked for you in New York as executive pastry chef."

Until you fired me.

"Now I'm back in my hometown, working right here in Wila as the executive pastry chef." She punctuated her introduction with a smile, relieved that her voice hadn't shook.

Liam nodded, his eyes lingering on hers. She held his gaze in a wordless game of visual chicken, daring him to be the first one to look away.

Or to ask her to leave the same way he had that night.

Finally, he blinked and moved on to the next person, sous chef Joe.

Jane stuffed her hands into the pockets of her white chef's coat and discovered that she was shaking. She sat like that for the duration of the introductions, which seemed to last an eternity.

When the last person had spoken, Liam said, "It's great to meet you all," then turned to Jane. "And it's nice to see you again, Jane... I'm sure you're all excellent at what you do, but I'm sure you'll understand why I need to meet with each of you individually and reinterview you for your jobs. Are there any questions?"

Liam had been blindsided when he'd walked in and seen Jane Clark sitting in the Wila dining room, looking just as surprised to see him as he was to see her.

He regretted the way he'd lost his temper when he'd fired her. Everyone in the kitchen had gone completely still, looking at him like he was a monster who might turn on them next, but her mistake had almost cost him everything he'd worked so hard to build.

Here they were again. Of all the restaurants in all the world, he had to walk into hers—or however that corny movie line went.

Why was he even thinking about corny movie lines at a time like this? He didn't have time to watch movies, much less quote them.

Jane Clark was a curveball. He'd have to deal with that later. For now, he needed to figure out what to do with the rest of the staff, who were glaring at him like he'd insulted their mothers. Reinterviewing for a job wasn't fun, and the stony faces staring back at him underscored the chore's unpopularity. But, really, it was simple. If they were good at what they did, they wouldn't have a problem. Attitude was everything. The current collective mood didn't bode well.

"Any questions?" he asked again.

You could've heard a pin drop.

"Anyone?"

It wasn't reverent silence from people who were hanging on his every word. He didn't want that kind of worship—he had no use for sycophants and hangers-on blowing sunshine at him. But he would've preferred a happy medium somewhere in between "you're our new best friend" and "go to hell." The vibe in the room was unmistakably closer to *go to hell*. Actually, it was more like *Who the hell are you to come in here and upset the natural order?*

He got it. Most people didn't like change. Especially when it had the ability to affect their livelihood. Still, this was more awkward than he'd expected.

"Look, I can see you're not thrilled with the idea of coming in and talking to me, but I'm not a bad guy."

He heard the words falling from his mouth and couldn't believe he felt compelled to sell himself. His usual tactic was to come in more heavy-handed and lighten up after he'd set the tone of expectation.

"I'm not looking for turnover for turnover's sake. I'm not looking to clean house here. I just need to know that we can all operate as a team. I'm not hard to get along with, despite what you might have heard." He paused and smiled, hoping they would see he was making a joke, but no one laughed. "I simply want you to do your job and do it right. Show me where you fit in as part of the team and you'll have no problem. Got it?"

Was it too much to ask? Of course not.

His gaze tacked back over to Jane Clark. To his surprise, she was one of the few who didn't look royally pissed.

God, what was he going to do about Jane Clark? He wasn't in the habit of giving second chances. But when he and Weathersby had been in the negotiating phase of this partnership, at first, Charles had wanted Liam to keep his staff intact. Liam had pushed back. He and Charles had finally met in the middle and agreed that everyone would have a one-month probationary period in which to prove themselves. Liam would not have agreed to that if he'd known Jane was part of the staff he'd inherit.

Now, she seemed to be the face of his challenge here.

Albeit a very pretty face. He looked away and blinked. Looks—pretty or otherwise—had nothing to do with whether he kept her on or not. If he ended up having to let her go, the last thing he needed was to give her reason to believe it had anything to do with anything other than her place on the team. This was strictly about her work performance—past and present—and the deal that he and Weathersby had penned.

Charles was staying on in more of a "front of the house" managerial role. Since his ties to Savannah ran deep, he would be the community contact, the PR department. Charles's standing in the community was one of the things that had made partnering with him to elevate Wila so attractive.

Liam had wanted to expand his portfolio of restaurants into the Southern region. He'd looked at various markets. Atlanta hadn't felt like the right fit. Miami was a different vibe altogether. Charleston had seemed closed to an outsider. Then Liam had met Charles at an Oscar Hurd Foundation dinner. As they'd talked, Liam happened to mention his love of Savannah and how he was looking to open a restaurant in the South. The germ of the idea for the partnership had been planted. But they'd had to iron out several wrinkles before they'd reached an agreement. The most stubborn one being retention of the current staff.

"So, you're saying you'd vouch for the entire staff? There are no problems?" Liam had asked. "Because I usually don't give second chances. Stupid mistakes are grounds for immediate dismissal. One and done."

Charles had frowned and for a moment Liam had feared that he would change his mind. "Nobody's perfect. That 'one and done' philosophy of yours seems like a good recipe for losing a lot of decent people—people with solid talent. Take it from someone who has been in this business longer than you've been alive—nobody's perfect, Liam. All I ask is that you treat my staff fairly. Give them a chance to prove themselves."

Liam would've preferred a less restrictive agreement but he could live with it. It stood to reason that those who couldn't stand the heat of his kitchen would leave of their own volition. If not, then he'd show them the door.

Since Liam was a man of his word, that meant he had no choice but to keep Jane Clark on board.

For now.

It rankled him, but it was his own fault. When

he'd looked at the employee roster, he hadn't put two and two together. If he'd realized *this* Jane Clark was *that* Jane Clark—the one who'd once worked for him at La Bula—he would have negotiated differently. Had Charles even known that Jane had worked for him in New York? Seems like he should've mentioned it.

Bottom line was that he had not done his homework. He had not looked into the employees before agreeing carte blanche to keep them on. That was Liam's mistake. He hated mistakes. Because they cost valuable time and money.

He would make damn sure that Jane's mistakes didn't put him in the same dangerous position that had given him no choice but to fire her. Even if he had to shadow her every move in his kitchen, he'd make sure she followed protocol. Because now that he was on board, she was baking in *his* kitchen. Again.

"Okay, if there are no questions," Liam said, "I'll post an appointment sign-up sheet in the break room. Please sign up today. I want to get this done before the weekend rush."

As he turned toward the kitchen, out of the corner of his eye, he saw a hand shoot up.

"Yes?" Liam said.

Those who had begun moving stopped to listen.

"Should we be worried?" the woman asked. "I mean about our jobs?"

The sharp teeth of irritation bit at him. He waited a moment before he spoke, his gaze piercing the young woman who'd asked the question.

"I don't know, uh…?" He gestured to her. "Tell me your name again."

"My name is Sally."

"I don't know, Sally. You know how well you do your job. You're the only one who can figure out if you need to be worried or not. I want good people. Do your job well and you shouldn't have to worry. It's simple."

He knew he sounded condescending, but that was exactly the type of inane question for which he had zero patience. Sally needed to understand that if she was going to continue to work at Wila.

"Any other questions?" he asked, mostly to see who else would expose themselves. "Anyone?"

No one raised a hand. Some glared at him.

This was an inauspicious start.

"Okay. I look forward to speaking with each of you individually."

Then he saw Jane Clark. The lone friendly face in the dining room. Actually, it was a look that registered somewhere between friendliness and pity.

Usually, he didn't care what anyone thought of

him. That had been his survival mode as a teenager living with his dad after his mother died. The loss had affected both of them deeply. Malcom Wright had lost his wife—the only woman he'd ever loved. Liam had lost his mom—an advocate, the person who had been the buffer between him and his father.

After she was gone, if Liam said black, his dad said white. The takeaway from those turbulent three years: Liam had learned to block out the sarcasm, the barbs and bullying that had come from a tough New York cop ashamed of his son because he wanted to cook for a living.

So, yeah. Growing a thick skin had been mandatory and it had served him well. The silent arrows slung by some of the staff would only hurt them in the long run.

So why did Jane Clark's warm smile feel like a lifeline?

He groaned inwardly and turned toward the kitchen.

"Chef?" Jane said.

He glanced back. "Yes?"

"Welcome to Savannah. Let me know if you need anything."

Liam blinked. Once. Twice.

The memory of Jane Clark's devastated face—

the way she'd looked the night he'd fired her—flashed through Liam's mind.

Of all the people who would have reason to take issue with him, it was Jane. Yet she was the only one who'd reached out.

"Thanks."

While he didn't need friends, he saw no reason to spit in a friendly face. There was something calming about her serene smile. It reminded him that there would be a learning curve here—on both sides. It would take time for him to get to know everyone, just as it would take time for even the best chefs and workers to adapt to his way of doing things. They'd just better not take too long if they knew what was good for them.

"Jane, let's talk for a moment," he said as most of the staff began to disperse. Her smile faded and he knew she was assessing him before closing the distance between them.

"Okay," she said.

"Come and take a walk with me," Liam said.

Jane frowned. "This isn't my interview, is it? Because I'm not ready and I have a thousand things to do before we open tonight. Unless you're not planning to give me an interview...but I hope you will because it wouldn't be fair. I've been doing a good job. Charles will vouch for me if you ask him. Charles?" she called.

His business partner had returned from his phone call and was deep in conversation with Sally, the hostess who'd asked the inane question and was now visibly upset. Charles seemed to be trying to calm her down. He held up a hand in Jane's direction, signaling he needed a minute.

"This isn't your interview," Liam said.

Jane swallowed so hard Liam saw her throat work. That's when he noticed something that looked like fear hidden behind the front she was trying like hell to project as she stood there, her chin slightly elevated and her arms crossed in front of her. Where was that smile she'd offered so freely just a minute ago?

"It's not?" She blinked again. "Oh. Okay. Good. Because I like my job. I just wanted you to know that." The earlier fear seemed to fade to something that was a little more in her control. "What do you need? I mean, like I said, I'm happy to help you however I can."

Even though she still looked nervous, he sensed something strong and determined in her. Something he hadn't noticed when she'd worked at La Bula.

Her long, dark brown hair was pulled back, accentuating her blue-gray eyes, high cheekbones and pretty heart-shaped face.

Why hadn't he noticed how attractive she was before now? Probably because he'd had his head down and his attention so focused on his work that he hadn't noticed much going on around him outside of business. And he was going to pretend like he hadn't noticed her looks now.

"I was wondering if you would be so kind as to show me around the kitchen?"

The request seemed to catch her by surprise.

Something flashed in her eyes that made them look sharp and silvery now.

"You're a partner. Charles hasn't shown you around the kitchen?"

Normally, sassiness like that would've bothered him, but it didn't. At least the woman had spunk…something else he hadn't witnessed in her before. Then again, he hadn't been around La Bula much. He'd been more focused on the PR part of the business, leaving his chefs to run the kitchen to his specifications while he traveled and made TV appearances.

He would be more hands-on in the month he would be in Savannah helping Charles transition the restaurant into the new vision the two of them had discussed.

"I've seen the kitchen," he said. "Only not while anyone was working. I want to see it through your eyes."

Suspicion narrowed her gaze. "I'm guessing you wouldn't ask me to show you around if you were going to fire me right away," she said. There was that sassy tone again. He wondered if it was a defense mechanism or if she figured she had nothing to lose. He liked this surprisingly stronger, sassier version of the woman who hadn't fought back when he'd fired her.

"Obviously, you weren't listening a few minutes ago," he countered. "I'm not firing anyone right away. Not until I've had a chance to talk to everyone. But if you'd rather not show me around, I'm happy to ask someone else to do it. It's up to you."

His eyes scanned the dining room. Charles had left. A group of servers was clustered at the hostess station, watching Jane and Liam talk. When they saw him looking, they turned away almost in unison and pretended to act busy. His ears should've been burning because he knew they were talking about him, and nice sentiments probably weren't part of the conversation. That was fine. That was the price of being the boss and the bad guy who came in and changed things.

"I'm happy to give you the grand tour," Jane

said. "But let's hurry. I don't have a lot of time. I'm already behind because of the meeting. In pastries, my day starts earlier than the rest of the kitchen. So meetings like that eat into my workday."

"I understand. Thanks for attending. It was important."

"Yes, it was. What kind of a team player would I be if I hadn't shown?"

He read between the lines and heard her unasked question. *Did I really have a choice?*

She hadn't. For that matter, he noticed, everyone had showed up. Weathersby had mentioned that several had even come in on their day off. It spoke volumes about the respect the staff had for Charles that no one had blown it off.

"I mixed up some bread dough and left it to rise before the meeting," she said. "If you don't mind, I need to punch it down and knead it a bit so it can get started on its second rise."

"Not a problem. Do you offer fresh bread every day?"

"Yes. Despite the anti-carb war going on in the world, I think our clientele would start a riot if we didn't offer fresh bread."

"Good to know. Do you work from an established house recipe?"

She shot him a look as if he'd asked an obvious question.

"No, the recipes are all mine. Originals I've come up with. Charles outsourced the restaurant's bread and most of the desserts before I came on board."

Liam raised his brows to show due reverence. At La Bula, the staff worked from established recipes—it was the only way to guarantee consistency. He had to hand it to Jane. She'd found a good way to slip in a tidbit about the valuable contribution she made—the creative change she'd implemented.

Noted.

As they entered the kitchen, Jane pointed to a wooden door, a stopper at the foot of the door propping it open.

"Did anyone tell you about the pantry?"

"No. Is there something I should know?"

Her lips quirked up into a smile. "Yes. It's a walk-in pantry. Always make sure the stopper stays in place when you're inside or you'll get locked in. There's something screwy with the latch. You can open it from out here, but not from the inside. Every once in a while, someone forgets—usually someone new. It's sort of become an initiation."

Liam frowned. "How long has it been like that?"

Jane shrugged. "For as long as I've been here."

Liam's frown deepened. "And no one's fixed it?"

Jane held up her hands. "Hey, don't shoot the messenger. I'm just telling you so you know."

Liam nodded. He hadn't meant to sound so critical. "Thank you. I appreciate the heads-up. It will be one of the first things I fix."

The kitchen was already a hive of activity as they prepped for the evening dinner service. Prep cooks were chopping the herbs, vegetables and protein for *mise en place*. Stocks, which would later be ladled into sauces, were simmering on flaming burners. Everyone seemed to know their job, each keeping their head down to do it.

As Liam followed Jane to her station, he inhaled the unmistakable smells of a commercial kitchen—a mix of diluted bleach, a mélange of spices, the tang of raw meat and the phantom scent of stale alcohol, which never seemed to go away no matter how much bleach.

Her station was a simple, stainless-steel table located in the corner at the far wall. Even though she'd come in early to get started, the area was neat and tidy, as if she'd cleaned up after herself before breaking for the meeting.

He watched her lift a large metal bowl and set it to the side of her station. After washing and drying her hands, she dusted the work area with flour and removed the plastic wrap from the bowl. She stuck her fist into the large dough ball and watched it deflate to half its size. She dumped it onto the floured surface and began the rhythmic work of kneading it into a shiny, elastic orb.

He would've understood if she'd left the area messy since she had work in progress. She hadn't known that he would be there today—unless she'd gotten wind about it from somewhere. He couldn't imagine who would've told her other than Charles. But she'd looked surprised when he'd walked in.

Cleanliness was mandatory. But as far as he was concerned, workday neatness was an unnecessary virtue as long as her baking mess didn't meander into other stations. His main concern was how the end product tasted.

He racked his brain trying to remember if any of the desserts Jane had made at La Bula had stood out—other than the rum baba, of course, and it had stood out for the wrong reasons.

"What else are you baking today?" he asked.

"Flourless chocolate cake. Profiteroles. Blackberry cobbler made with local berries and served with homemade vanilla bean ice cream," she said. "And rum baba."

She didn't crack a smile. He wondered if she'd added it to the menu for his sake. He hoped so. The Wila menu changed every day because Charles said the executive chef always planned what he served around what was fresh. That was a concept Liam respected and planned to keep, possibly putting even more emphasis on the farm-to-table aspect.

The restaurant was closed on Sundays and Mondays, and during the time he and Charles had been trying to decide if they would work as partners, he'd met Charles at Wila on those days.

He'd come in for dinner, of course, and Charles had done his best to ensure the kitchen hadn't known he was testing the place. Judging from the looks on their faces this morning, the entire staff had had no idea he'd been there before.

It wasn't a surprise that he had slipped by the front-of-the-house staff unnoticed. While it had served his purpose for due diligence, the oversight made him wonder just how aware the kitchen staff was of what was happening in the dining room on a nightly basis. He made a mental note to figure that out by asking a few pointed questions during the interviews, but first, he wanted to see the kitchen through Jane's eyes.

Chapter Two

Jane stayed at the restaurant later than usual to make sure everything was on point before she clocked out. When she arrived home at the Forsyth Galloway Inn, the bed-and-breakfast that had been in their family for six generations and where she'd been living since she'd returned to Savannah, she was happy to find her sister Ellie was there.

Ellie had just finished with one of her art journaling classes that she was teaching, a new amenity they offered to guests of the Forsyth. The classes were also open to the community if space permitted.

Ellie had been an elementary school art teacher

in Atlanta before she'd moved back to Savannah permanently after marrying the love of her life. Since returning, she'd given up teaching to help their mom and grandmother at the Forsyth Galloway Inn. As Savannah was such an artistic and picturesque city, the three women had come up with the idea of offering art and architecture tours and art classes at the inn. It was a way to entice new guests to choose the Forsythe Galloway Inn over the plethora of B and B options in the area. So far it was working. So well, in fact, that now, her mother and grandmother, Gigi, wanted to move on to phase two of their plan: opening a tearoom.

Jane was staying in one of the guest houses on the grounds of the inn until she decided what she wanted to do. It was her mom and grandmother's way of compensating her for the tearoom consulting. Jane suspected that the other, less-talked-about part of their plan was that if Jane stayed close and became invested enough in the progress of the tearoom, she might eventually take over its management in a similar way that Ellie had taken over the art tours and classes.

Dedicating herself full-time to an uncharted venture wasn't in the cards for Jane right now. She needed a steady income to pay back the student loan for culinary school and other debt that had racked up when she was in New York.

Living in the city had been the fulfillment of a lifelong dream. It had also been expensive and her salary certainly hadn't made her rich. In fact, it had been just enough to get by living with a roommate in a tiny two-bedroom apartment in the West Village. After she'd been fired, she'd been determined to find another position, but after three months of unemployment depleted her savings and ran up her credit cards, she'd had no choice but to come home.

Her thirtieth birthday was right around the corner. It was humbling to find herself back in the place she'd sworn she'd left behind forever. After a lot of soul-searching, she'd come to realize she could view the glass as half-empty: she was a failure who couldn't make it work and had no choice but to return home, her tail between her legs. Or half-full: her family had welcomed her home with open arms; Charles had given her a good job with a good salary. She was not only living within her means, she had rebuilt her savings and was paying off her debt at a pace she never thought would be possible. At least, not in New York. When she counted her blessings, she was truly fortunate.

And now there was Liam. With one sweep of

his hand, he could wreak havoc in her life—again. However, this time he wouldn't have the power to devastate her.

She'd had other offers. Of course, accepting another offer at a salary commensurate to what she was now making would probably mean moving again. Charles had created the position for her and, after swearing she wouldn't return to New York, she was just starting to figure things out. She had just decided she was happy here.

Sure, she would survive if she had to move again, but damn it, this was starting to feel like a pattern. Just when she got comfortable, Liam Wright showed up and knocked down everything she'd worked so hard to build.

She blinked away the thought. She wasn't going think about him now. Why would she let Liam Wright darken this otherwise happy moment when she was preparing to have tea with her sister and talk about happy things? Being surrounded by family was one of the many blessings of being back in Savannah.

What her family lacked in financial resources, they made up for in love and emotional support. That was something money couldn't buy. One of the things she wouldn't be able to recreate if she had to move again.

She took the kettle off the stove and poured the water into the white teapot that held loose leaf chamomile tea in its round belly. Jane placed it on the trestle table, next to the pretty, floral china cups and saucers Ellie had already gathered and placed there. She also noted the two silver tea strainers and the hourglass tea timer that would silently alert them to the moment the tea had steeped to perfection.

Jane took a seat at the big table in the kitchen and noticed her sister had a certain look on her face.

For a fleeting moment, she wondered if Ellie had heard about Liam's unexpected arrival. Maybe Charles had told Gigi and Gigi had told Ellie? News traveled fast in this family.

"What's that look about?" Jane placed the strainers across the cups and did her best to look blasé despite the way her heart hammered against her breastbone. Talking about the changes at Wila would make it too real. Even though the changes Liam wanted to make would hit eventually, it would be nice if she could live in denial one more night.

"Daniel and I have been talking about baby names," Ellie said.

Jane sloshed the tea that she was pouring into

Ellie's cup. "Wait a minute. What?" She set down the pot and focused on her sister. "Are you...?" Jane pointed to Ellie's stomach. Okay, so, clearly not everything was about her and her job. Thank God.

When Ellie covered her mouth as if to contain her glee and nodded, Jane jumped up and hugged her.

"We just found out. You're the first person we've told. So don't say anything to mom and Gigi. Or Kate."

"Especially not Kate," Jane seconded. Kate was their youngest sister. She couldn't keep a secret if her life depended on it. "I am so happy for you, and I'm beyond thrilled that you told me first. I feel pretty special."

Ellie and Daniel were having a baby.

Jane was a jumble of feelings. Mostly good... No. It was *all good*. Ellie was her sister—the middle sister. Last summer, she'd tied the knot with the love of her life, Daniel Quindlen. It had been a hard-won happily-ever-after because they'd started out as sworn enemies before they'd realized the strong feelings they had for each other was really love. Ellie liked to say that it proved that there was a thin line between love and hate. And love had triumphed. Now their fairy tale had gotten even better with this delicious morsel of news.

Even if Ellie's marriage and pending mother-hood underscored exactly how Jane was hopelessly married to her job—and her job wasn't faithful all the time—it didn't mean she wasn't happy for her sister. Despite the scratchy feel of envy that rubbed her like a too small wool sweater.

Ellie sipped her tea and looked dreamy in that way that only a newlywed expectant mother could look. "It was a surprise, but we are so happy."

"Of course. What's not to love about it?" said Jane. "I can't wait to be an auntie. At least one of us will make Gigi happy. Better you than me."

Gigi, whose real name was Wiladean Boudreaux, was their grandmother and the matriarch of the family. She and Jane shared a birthday. On the same day, Jane would turn thirty and Gigi would turn eighty-five. Gigi kept telling her three granddaughters all she wanted for this milestone birthday was for all three of them to be happily married and for at least one of them to make her a great-Gigi. It looked as if she might have to settle for part of her wish.

Gigi liked to brag that she was responsible for bringing the stubborn couple of Ellie and Daniel together, through some strategic matchmaking.

Jane and her youngest sister, Kathryn, had realized that if they let Gigi bask in that glory, she would forgive them for being persistently single. Neither one of them had any prospects on the horizon. Even though both would love to find their soul mate, neither was desperate to make it happen. Not even for Gigi, whom they both loved dearly.

Since their grandmother was fresh off the Ellie and Daniel success, she had been sporadic about turning her penchant for matchmaking on Jane. Of course, Gigi had tried to set her up a couple of times since she'd been back in Savannah, but it hadn't worked out. Jane's full focus had been on getting settled and advancing her career. Now, with things up in the air at Wila for the next month, Jane didn't need any distractions.

She'd learned the hard way that restaurant work wasn't conducive to building healthy romantic relationships. Shoot, it wasn't even conducive for meeting anyone. She was stuck in the kitchen all day, working when most people were playing. On her days off—Sunday and Monday—she was exhausted and all she wanted to do was recharge. The last thing she needed was the pressure of nurturing a brand-new romance. After the first two disastrous setups, Jane had asked Gigi to stop, reminding her that any time she spent dating would be time away from planning the tearoom.

It worked like magic because Gigi had stopped. Just like that.

Even though Jane was grateful for this rare instance when her grandmother listened, Jane had to admit that seeing how happy Ellie and Daniel were made her a wee bit wistful.

She was happy for her sister, but she couldn't deny there was an emptiness inside her that not even all the accolades in the restaurant world could fill.

"Names! Tell me the names you're considering," Jane insisted.

"If we have a girl, we want to name her Willow, as a nod to Gigi, of course. Don't you think she'd love that?"

"You're gunning for granddaughter of the year, aren't you?"

Jane raised her teacup to Ellie. Her sister rolled her eyes and smiled. "Maybe. And if we have a boy, we were thinking of the name Liam."

Jane choked on her tea.

Ellie frowned as Jane dragged the cloth napkin across her mouth in the pretense of wiping away drips of tea, but, really, she was trying to hide her utter horror.

"What's wrong?" Ellie asked. "Why don't you like the name Liam?"

Jane snorted and gave her head a quick shake. She sipped her tea again, trying to sooth her tickling throat, irritated when the warm beverage nearly came out her nose.

"Tell me." Ellie reached across the table and nudged Jane's arm. "I don't want you recoiling every time you see your nephew. You'll give the poor little guy a complex."

"I won't recoil. My tea just went down the wrong pipe."

Ellie studied her dubiously. "Are you sure?"

"If you and Daniel love that name, by all means, keep it on your list." Ellie was still giving her the side-eye. Jane knew she needed to change the subject fast.

"Is it hard picking names? I would imagine teaching for so many years, you'd start associating names with certain kids. Did that eliminate a bunch of possibilities?"

"I see what you're doing there. Don't change the subject, Jane. What's wrong with the name Liam?"

"Nothing is wrong with the name Liam."

Ellie frowned at her. "I have all night. I hope you wouldn't make a pregnant woman sit up and pry it out of you. I need my sleep more than ever now."

She and her sister had such a bond that sometimes it was as if they could read each other's minds.

"Okay. Okay." Jane scrunched up her face and then covered it with her hands. "It just brings back bad memories. That's all. But I mean it, if you and Daniel like the name, please don't take it off your list on my account."

Ellie pursed her lips and squinted at Jane. "I don't remember you dating a Liam."

"I didn't date a Liam," Jane said.

Ellie's eyes got big. "Did you have a one-night stand with some hot, hunky bad boy named Liam and now remembering it makes you feel naughty?"

The flash of an image of Liam Wright, in bed and covered only by a white sheet and a smattering of tattoos, flashed through Jane's head. The thought made her squirm. It was ridiculous. She had no idea if Liam Wright had tattoos.

And she didn't want to know. *Sort of—*

"Don't be absurd." Jane rolled her eyes. She wished it was something so simple and sexy. But not with Liam. At least it would've meant she'd been in charge of the situation. But the sad truth was, she'd never been naughty like that a single night in her life.

"Then why are you blushing?"

"Because you're embarrassing. *That's embarrassing.*" Thinking about her boss, the one who'd fired her, the one who would never give her the time of day because he only dated supermodels, was embarrassing. How was she supposed to not see that image of him the next time she looked at him?

"For your information," Jane said, "I've never had a one-night stand in my entire life."

Ellie looked incredulous. "Not when you lived in New York City?"

"Nope. I had a boyfriend for a while and then I was just too busy to meet anyone. Restaurant hours aren't exactly conducive for meeting people."

"Maybe we need to get you laid," Ellie said.

"And how long do you think it would take for that to get back to Gigi? She'd perform the shotgun wedding herself."

"You're right. But that's beside the point. Tell me why you're judging the name we've chosen for our sweet baby boy."

"Given our family's track record, you'll probably have a girl."

"Daniel has a brother. We might not. And now our poor baby boy doesn't have a name."

"Ugh." Jane braced her elbows on the table and buried her face in her hands. "Okay." She peered up at her sister. "You really don't remember?"

"If I remembered, do you think I'd be asking you?"

Jane sighed. "This is just too weird."

"What is? Tell me."

Obviously, Ellie wasn't going to let this go.

"Remember Liam Wright who owns La Bula?"

Ellie stared back at her blankly for a few beats.

Jane didn't remember the name of the principal at the school where Ellie had worked. It shouldn't be surprising that her sister didn't remember Liam's name. She wasn't a foodie and she didn't watch reality TV. The fact that Liam had won *America's Best Chef* and had made numerous appearances on cooking shows meant nothing to her.

"He's the guy who fired me…? The reason I'm back here…?"

Ellie's mouth formed a perfect *O* before she could cover it with her hand. "Oh, yikes, Jane, that's right. I am so sorry."

Ellie was one of the few people who knew the whole story and Jane had sworn her to secrecy. Obviously, she'd taken that pledge to heart.

"It's not a big deal," Jane said. "Except that

today—today of all days for you to mention the name Liam—Liam Wright showed up at Wila."

"What?" Ellie's mouth fell open again. "Why? He lives in New York City. What is he doing here?"

Jane shook her head, still half hoping she would shake herself awake and discover that it really was all a bad dream. "He's Charles's new business partner. We found out this morning in a staff meeting."

"You've got to be kidding me. I can't believe Charles has taken on a business partner. Most important, though, what does that mean for you?" Ellie grimaced as if bracing for bad news.

"We all have to reinterview for our jobs, but Liam said he won't be making any changes for a month. Apparently, that was one of Charles's non-negotiable stipulations for the partnership. Liam has to give the current team a fighting chance. But that's short-term. We have a month to prove ourselves. After that, it doesn't mean he has to keep us."

Saying the words out loud made Jane's stomach hurt. She couldn't beat the situation she had now, living in the guest cottage in exchange for helping her mom and Gigi was a win-win for all of them. With the decreased expenses, she'd been able to double up on her student loan payments, which meant she would be debt-free within the next two years. By that time, the tearoom should be up and running and, if all went according to plan, turning a profit. If she lost her job and had to move, it would set everyone back.

"I'm sorry," said Ellie. "No wonder the name bothers you so much. Now it bothers me, too. Don't worry, we'll pick another one."

"No!" Jane protested. "Please don't take it off the list. I'm over it. I promise it won't bother me. In fact, if you named a sweet baby boy Liam, you would be doing all guys in the world named Liam a favor by rebranding it. Because your son would redeem the name, no doubt."

Ellie sighed. "It was so insensitive of me not to remember. I know how it feels to lose your job." Ellie's job as an art teacher had been eliminated at the end of last year's school year. While it had been a hard blow when it happened, the county had eventually called and offered her another position as a curriculum resource professional. But by the time she'd gotten the call, she had already decided to stay in Savannah. She was in love.

"I appreciate your empathy, but it's not really the same thing, Ellie. You chose to walk away from the job. I was fired."

Heat prickled Jane's cheeks at the memory. She'd never been fired from anything in her life until Liam Wright had lost his temper and sacked her right in the middle of the kitchen—in front of everyone. The real rub: it hadn't even been her fault. Her assistant had mistakenly used salt instead of sugar in the rum baba.

They had been in the weeds that night and Jane had been so busy trying to keep up with the dessert orders that she hadn't tasted each batch of rum baba that her assistant had produced. When the tainted cakes were served not only to guests dining at La Bula that night, but also to Eduardo Sanchez, the editor of *Food Connoisseur* magazine, the onus had been on Jane.

In that regard, she had failed miserably. She'd let herself down as much as she had Liam. Because it wasn't the kind of impression you wanted to make on the editor of a magazine considered the bible of the food industry. A review from that publication could make or break a restaurant.

So, just as her mistake ultimately tainted Liam and La Bula, the assistant's mistake was on Jane's head.

It wouldn't have changed anything to throw her pastry assistant under the bus. Though it would've been nice if Liam hadn't berated Jane in front of God and everyone before he'd sent her packing.

"I'm still surprised you're actually considering

boy names, given it's your duty to produce a female heir to continue the family legacy."

The Forsyth Galloway Inn had been passed down through six generations of females on Gigi's side of the family.

"My duty?" Ellie scoffed. "I don't recall you and Kate being released from the task and the responsibility being placed on me."

"At the rate Kate and I are going, it may all be on your shoulders, Ellie. Don't let us down."

"I'll do my best, but I can't guarantee Daniel and I will have a girl. Did you ever wonder what would happen if all of us only had boys? What happens to the inn if we don't deliver a female heir? Gigi won't even discuss the possibility."

"She probably has a magic potion that she'll slip into your food that will make you have a girl."

Ellie shrugged. "I wouldn't put it past her. I wouldn't really mind. Growing up with sisters wasn't so bad. You've always been my best friend as much as my sister. It could've been a lot worse."

They were both quiet for a moment. Jane watched her sister sip her tea.

"Do you think Charles would really let Liam fire you? He's been like a grandfather to us. I mean...could Liam really do that? If they're partners, I would think that Charles would be your best advocate. I'd think he'd consider you pretty sacred given how he feels about Gigi."

Though no one had ever discussed it, it wasn't a secret that Charles was crazy about their grandmother.

"They're not equal partners," Jane said. "I don't know the ins and outs of the logistics, but apparently Charles only holds a small share of Wila now, just enough to keep him in the game. Liam is majority owner. Once again, my fate is in his hands."

Chapter Three

Having her hands in bread dough helped Jane center herself. It steadied her nerves. Because she was nervous having signed up for the first interview.

The following day, just as she'd done before the meeting when Charles had introduced Liam, she'd come in early to get the bread started before her one-on-one. This time it was to take her nerves out on the dough as much as it was to jump-start the day.

After Ellie left, Jane had updated and printed her résumé. Then she'd spent most of the night tossing and turning, mulling over questions she wanted to ask Liam and thinking about how she would answer his questions. Especially the burning inquiry he was bound to ask. What happened that night at La Bula?

She'd decided she wouldn't bring it up unless he asked.

She shove-stretched the dough with the heel of her hand and gave it a quarter twist before folding it over and repeating the rhythmic process.

He didn't ask then. Of course, he'll ask now. Won't he?

Shove, twist, fold. Shove, twist, fold.

Unless he waits for me to bring it up.

Should she?

No. She decided she would not. She had moved on. She'd even made the most perfect batch of rum baba for last night's dinner. Each cake perfectly formed and extra delicious.

She'd tasted every single batch because— Well…*ha, ha, ha.* She tried very hard not to make the same stupid mistake twice.

Liam had tasted the cake, too.

He hadn't said anything to her, but she'd seen him put one of the cakes on a small red plate that was one of the odds and ends that had turned up in the kitchen. She'd watched him cut into the pastry and poke at it with his finger, testing the crumb.

Then, he'd hesitantly forked up a small bite. She'd looked away because she hadn't wanted to know what he'd thought. The batch had the right ingredients. She loved her rum baba...

Besides, she'd been too busy to worry about Liam's critique of the classic French dessert. At the same time Liam was eating cake, Charles had presented her with a special order of chocolate Grand Marnier soufflé. The temperamental dessert hadn't been on this month's menu, but it was one of the recipes Charles had let her introduce when she'd first arrived. Very occasionally, someone would ask if she could whip one up. Last night, it had been a special request from Charles on behalf of his friends.

Of course, when the guests at the tables next to Charles's friends saw the soufflé in all its grandeur, it had started a trend of copycat orders.

By the time she'd conquered the soufflé frenzy, there was no sight of Liam. Only an empty red plate with a fork balanced across it in the four o'clock-ten o'clock position set at the corner of her workstation.

Jane chose to believe the empty plate was his way of complimenting her.

In addition to the special requests, they'd been busier than usual last night, working in some of the guests whose reservations had to be canceled for the week they'd be closed for training. The hostesses had spent the afternoon calling every guest who had booked a dinner for next week, trying to reschedule. Judging by the behind-the-hand comments and behind-Liam's-back eye rolls, it had been a monumental effort.

Jane couldn't imagine how any type of training could be worth closing the restaurant for a week, but it wasn't her call. Like most of her coworkers who wanted to keep their jobs, she was determined to make it through this interview the best she could and prove she was a team player who was good at her job.

She was washing her hands after covering the bread dough and leaving it for its final rise when she looked up to see Liam entering the kitchen.

He was wearing a royal-blue-and-black print button-down tucked into jeans. His dark hair was still wet from his morning shower. As he walked toward her, the mental picture that had commandeered her thoughts last night—Liam lying in bed amid the mussed bedsheets—intruded again.

She sighed.

Girl, that is so inappropriate. What's wrong with you?

She dropped her gaze to the towel she'd grabbed

off the counter and concentrated on thoroughly drying her hands—one finger at a time. Anything to get that image of Liam out of her head. What he was like in bed was the last thing she needed to think about when she was preparing to interview for her life.

This was nothing like the speaker's trick of imagining people in their underwear before addressing a crowd. Imagining your boss naked and in bed—as your first one-night-stand—was altogether different.

Jane swallowed hard and realized that telling herself not to think about it was just like telling someone not to picture a pink elephant.

"Good morning," he said.

"Morning, chef." She forced her gaze to his face, but she was having a hard time looking him in the eyes and she needed to get over that before they sat down together.

"Thanks for being the first to sign up," he said.

She forced herself to lock gazes with him, which made her stomach do a slow roll. Why did he have to be so good-looking? Why did she have to notice? Worse yet, why was her body betraying her and acting like she was attracted to him?

No! No! No! No! Stop it right now.

She tossed the towel onto her workstation, lifted

her chin and put her hands on her hips. "Someone had to go first." She'd read an article about body language that suggested when you feel small or out of control, physically making yourself bigger— the bigger the better—helped a person feel more in control.

"I figured it might as well be me. Would you like some coffee? I just brewed a fresh pot."

"I would love a cup," he said. "How did you know?"

"It's one of my skills." She tucked the folder containing her résumé under her arm and grabbed the copper travel mug of coffee, her fourth cup this morning. "I should've added occasional mind reader to my list of professional skills on my résumé."

"I'd better be careful then." He slanted a smile at her that held plenty of fodder for overthinking before he turned and headed toward the office.

Did he mean that in a good way or a bad way?

His sexy smile was almost flirtatious. But then again, the colossal mistake that had caused him to fire me still stands between us.

Stop! You'd better start remembering all the brilliant answers you came up with last night instead of sleeping.

Her mouth went dry as she realized that every

single, smart, witty response had evaporated like a berry glaze she'd left on the burner too long.

Liam gestured to the seat on the other side of Charles's desk. Dutifully, she sat. As she watched him gather a yellow legal pad and a blue ballpoint pen, she sipped her coffee and centered herself.

Liam was her boss. His only interest was whether she knew her choux from her shortcrust and how well she could whip up batches of Palmier and profiteroles… And, of course, the rum baba.

Enough with the rum baba. You've proved yourself.

"How about if we start off with you telling me a little bit about yourself?"

That was easy enough. She gave him the extended version of what she'd said yesterday when he'd had everyone introduce themselves.

The next two questions were easy, too.

"When you're not at work, where do you go for great pastry?"

"Leonie's." She waxed poetic about the virtue of Leonie's *bossche bols*.

"*Bossche bols?* What's that?"

She made a guttural sound that she hadn't intended be so…animalistic. Then she cleared her throat. "It's pure pleasure. Essentially, it's a big profiterole made from the flakiest choux pastry you've ever tasted in your life and filled with the lightest whipped cream and, finally, coated entirely with dark Belgian chocolate. God, it's absolutely orgas—"

She closed her lips just in time—right before she'd said the word. Actually, it wasn't just orgasmic. It was better than sex.

Her cheeks burned.

Liam looked up from where he'd been scribbling. "It's that good, huh?"

"Oh, my God, you have no idea—"

"Why is it better than yours?"

She blinked at him. "Excuse me?"

He raised both of his brows and he looked a little irritated. "Why is Leonie's *bossche bols* better than yours? Why should I keep you on if she's the best? Should I hire her?"

Now she remembered why she hadn't like him very much when she'd worked for him. That challenging, smug, arrogant, sexy—

No! Not sexy.

Well, yeah, he is sexy.

She leaned in. "First of all, *bossche bols* is not on Wila's menu. That's why I go to Leonie's for it. Second, good luck with hiring Leonie for my job because Leonie isn't a person. *Leonie's* is a bakery. It's owned by Doug Niedermeyer. Doug does a wonderful business. So, I'm sure he's good where he is. I mean you could try to get him. But I'd be willing to wager that he'd turn you down."

This time Liam's right brow shot up. "Really?"

She nodded.

"You like to gamble?"

"What?"

"You said you'd be willing to wager."

Now he was making her mad. "Don't be ridiculous. That's a figure of speech. Can we just get back to the interview?"

He laughed and she noticed that he had a scar on the left side of his upper lip. She felt her cheeks burn again and tried to console herself by writing it off to the stress of the interview, which felt like it was going downhill faster than a broken case of lemons.

He scribbled more notes then said, "The kitchen is a busy, fast-paced, often stressful environment. How do you cope with stress, Jane?"

A shiver shimmied through her at the sound of her name in his mouth.

She uncrossed her legs and recrossed them in the other direction.

"I'm pretty even-tempered. It takes a lot for me to lose my cool, which is an asset in an environment like that. But when I need an outlet, I write in my notebook. That's where I write thoughts and observations about recipes and methods. It's where I work through a lot of things. I can leave it all on the page."

"What's the biggest mistake you've ever made?"

He gave her a knowing look.

Okay, here we go.

She'd nearly forgotten about this question, about the rum baba incident. Obviously, he hadn't. He'd been playing with her before he went in for the kill.

She didn't have to play right into his hand.

"Personal or professional?"

She knew darn good and well he didn't want to hear about her personal life. This was a job interview. She could read between the lines. He wanted her to explain herself. To ask for absolution for *the incident.* She didn't have to be a mind reader to know that.

Especially because now, he was frowning. "I'm talking about mistakes you've made in the kitchen. Or in the restaurant." He gestured to her as if saying, *fess up* or *get on with it.*

Okay, sure, she'd screwed up. But she didn't consider what had happened to be the *biggest* mistake she'd ever made.

She held his gaze. "The biggest mistake I've

ever made was firing someone without giving them a second chance—"

His sigh interrupted her.

"I'm not finished," she said. "Please let me finish."

He gave a curt nod.

"After I fired this person, I realized I'd been rash. Later on, I got the opportunity to give him a second chance. I rehired him and he went on to be very successful."

"He was successful because *you* rehired him?"

"You're missing the point," Jane said.

"No, I get the point that you're trying to make," Liam said as he scribbled more notes on his legal pad. "I hear you loud and clear. I didn't ask for a hypothetical situation. I asked for you to tell me about an actual mistake."

"The person was Bruce Tremayne."

Liam looked up.

"You once fired Bruce Tremayne?" His voice was flat.

"Yeah, it was before I worked for you at La Bula. I rehired him because he's a damn good pastry chef. You do know that he went on to be one of the most successful pastry chefs in—"

"I know Bruce very well. I'm going to follow up

with him. Did you list him as a reference?" Liam picked up her résumé and skimmed it.

"Knock yourself out. In fact, I'd love for you to ask Bruce for a reference. Although I didn't list him. I didn't work for him. He worked for me. But you know what? I'm happy to give you his number if you need it." She reached for her phone.

"I have his number," Liam said. "Why don't I call him right now?"

Jane nodded. "I hope you will."

He held her gaze as he picked up his phone. What? Did he think he was calling her bluff? When she didn't react, he pressed a few buttons.

"Bruce? Liam Wright."

In a matter of seconds, Jane could hear the muted tones of a male voice on the other end of the call as Liam and Bruce exchanged pleasantries. Since the phone was pressed to Liam's ear, she could make out the general congenial tones of the conversation, but not every specific word.

They made small talk for a few minutes and then Liam said, "So, Bruce, I'm down in Savannah working on a new restaurant. My executive pastry chef here is someone named Jane Clark. She mentioned she knows you."

Liam paused, no doubt giving Bruce a chance to say Jane who? But from what Jane could make out, he didn't ask. Based on what she could hear, Bruce's tone sounded warm and friendly.

"Would you hire her?"

For the next minute or two, Bruce did most of the talking. His tone sounded enthusiastic. She was glad Liam hadn't told Bruce she was sitting there. She wanted him to speak candidly. It was vindicating, really.

Yes, very vindicating.

Liam nodded, his handsome face stoic as a statue.

Why did he have to be so damned handsome? Her eyes tracked back to the scar above his lip. She wondered how he'd gotten it.

She waited for him to look at her so she could give him the old *I-told-you-so* raised brow. But he kept his gaze focused on a spot somewhere over her left shoulder.

"Oh, she fired you, huh?"

He finally slanted a look in her direction.

She crossed her arms and pursed her lips, giving him the stink eye.

"So, you worked for her twice?" More nodding. "Okay, man, thanks. I appreciate the input. I'll keep what you said in mind. Good to talk to you."

He hung up and shifted his gaze back to the paper, focusing on the legal pad in front of him, stoic again as he scribbled some things down. Jane couldn't tell from his expression what he was thinking.

Figuring she had nothing to lose, she said, "Well?"

It took a couple of beats, but he finally looked up.

"How do you manage your time when you receive multiple dessert orders at once?"

He was moving on to the next question?

"Wait a minute," Jane said.

She should've let it go, but she wasn't ready to move on from the phone call. If he was moving on to the next question, clearly it meant that Bruce said only good things about her. It wouldn't hurt for Liam to repeat them.

"Excuse me?" he said.

"What did Bruce say?"

He furrowed his brow. "He said you are one of the best pastry chefs on the East Coast and if I didn't hire you, he would."

A jolt of satisfaction shot through her. She had to bite the insides of her cheeks to keep from smiling.

Score!

Jane: one. Liam: zero.

"Is that so?" she asked.

He nodded. "If things don't work out here, at least you have a job in San Francisco."

"I don't want to move to San Francisco," she said. "I'm perfectly happy right here in Savannah. I'd like to stay here."

"Why?"

He set down his pen and looked at her. This time it felt different. It was as if he was really looking at her rather than looking through her.

"I came back after—" She stopped herself from saying it just in time. Since he hadn't mentioned firing her, she wasn't going to bring it up. No. Instead, she was going to hold fast to how much she loved being back. "I'm happy to be back, and I'd like to stay for a while. It's my hometown. I'm enjoying the change."

He arched his brow and, for a moment, she was afraid he might bring up the firing incident. But he didn't.

"You're from here?"

She nodded.

"When you were in New York, I didn't realize Savannah was your home. You'll have to give me some pointers on navigating the city."

Something passed between them, but Jane couldn't figure out exactly what it was.

Liam Wright had a reputation for having a big

ego, but was he so arrogant that he would fire her a second time and then think he could pump her for the inside scoop on Savannah?

"Listen, chef, I know this city intimately. Savannah is not like other places. It's a quirky big little town. I'm happy to help you get acquainted."

"Good to know. Now, I know who to come to with questions."

"Does that mean I passed the interview?" she asked. "If I'm going to be your go-to person for all things Savannah, I suppose you'll have to keep me on board."

He looked at her with piercing brown eyes that were as dark as the black coffee they were drinking, but the rest of his face was unreadable.

Is he this intense in bed?

Stop!

She felt heat prickle the sensitive skin at the base of her cleavage. She willed the flush to stop there.

"Bruce is the second person who says you're the best pastry chef in the southeast. Charles claims you're the best pastry chef Wila's has ever seen."

Jane bit back a smile. She was the only executive pastry chef Wila's had ever had. Charles created the position for her.

"Apparently, he hasn't tasted your rum baba."

"Excuse me? You tasted my rum baba last night. You finished it. So, you must've enjoyed it."

"I did. What I meant was he hasn't tasted your special recipe."

It took every ounce of self-control not to tell him the mix-up hadn't been her fault. Defending herself now wouldn't serve any purpose. But wait—had Liam just admitted that he'd enjoyed her cake?

"You'll need to bake more for me. Three or four of your specialties that show off your skills. Maybe even a batch of *bossche bols*. The others will have to cook, too. So don't think you're special."

He looked up from the legal pad and the left side of his mouth quirked, making her notice that sexy scar again.

There it was. That feeling. That strange chemistry that turned her mind into a messy stew of emotions. Her heart was hammering and her stomach had tied itself into one big knot.

She was a mess. This couldn't be happening. She could not have a crush on Liam Wright.

Because that was a recipe for disaster.

By the end of the day, Liam lost Wila's executive chef, forcing Liam to fill that role for the night.

Even though most executive chefs had culinary

voices of their own, it was imperative that Wila's chef restaurant that prepare *Liam's* food to *his* standards. Because after they reopened, people would come to Liam's restaurants to eat his food.

The guy that Charles had in place had been too territorial, too bristly. The first thing out of the guy's mouth when he sat down for his interview was, "Why did you buy an established restaurant if you were going to come in and change things?" It was downhill from there, ending with the guy's resignation.

Liam had tried to explain that people would continue to come to Wila for the quality experience, but now that his name would be attached to the restaurant, they would come for his food. Even with that, the guy couldn't understand why he couldn't keep cooking his own food his way. He'd made it clear he had no intention of trying to be a team player.

Second only to perfect food, Liam insisted on no drama in the kitchen. Drama took the focus away from the food and sometimes ate into the guest's dining experience. There would be none of that here.

A couple of line cooks had followed the chef out of loyalty—just as well. He wasn't there to babysit and he had no intentions of coddling a group of adults.

A server had used the interview as an opportunity to give notice because she was going back to school, but other than that, the interviews went well.

What surprised him the most was how strong Jane Clark was turning out to be. Since he'd arrived yesterday, he was seeing a completely different side of her. Shades of Jane he hadn't known when she'd worked for him before.

The night he'd fired her, she'd looked devastated. She hadn't tried to explain herself or to ask for a second chance. She'd pierced him with those distraught gray eyes and then gathered her things and left. Of course, he'd preferred it that way because he didn't want excuses. That night there hadn't been time for her to explain. He'd had to shift into damage control mode to try to save the review.

The editor had left. Dinner, of course, had been on the house. And, temporarily, egg had been on Liam's face, but thanks to some smooth public relations and a dozen perfectly executed rum baba cakes prepared and hand-delivered to the *Food Connoisseur* magazine offices the next morning, Eduardo

Sanchez had conveniently forgotten to mention the unpalatable final impression of the meal.

Maybe Jane's new strength stemmed from being on her home turf. Maybe he'd just been too damn busy to see *this* Jane Clark in New York, but he liked this stronger, spunkier side of her.

Maybe she was right. Maybe sometimes it's worth giving a second chance. Time would tell, but first, he needed to have a wrap-up meeting with the staff before the dinner service started.

He walked to the middle of the kitchen and gave two loud claps of his hands. "Could I have everyone's attention, please?" It took a moment, but eventually everyone stopped what they were doing. All eyes were on him.

"Thanks for helping me get the interviews behind us. Could everyone meet me in the dining room in twenty minutes—uh, let's say one fifteen—for a short meeting? I know you have a lot to do before we open tonight, but since tonight is the last night we will be open before the week of training begins, we need to touch base."

"Can you take a break?"

Jane turned around to find Robin Howell standing at her workstation.

"Hey," Jane said as she glanced at her watch. It

was one o'clock. "Who let you out? Shouldn't you be wrapping up the lunch rush?"

Robin, Jane's best friend, was the chef/owner of the Pig and Whistle, a sandwich shop on Abercorn Street. Being able to see her on a regular basis was one of the perks of returning to Savannah. When Jane started feeling down on herself, she reminded herself of that.

"I sneaked out for a couple of minutes to come visit you."

Robin's strangely timed surprise appearance, during the lunch rush, coupled with the way she kept glancing around the busy kitchen, made Jane instantly suspicious. The Pig was a favorite lunch spot. Usually, Robin couldn't be smoked out of the shop during prime hours.

Jane narrowed her eyes. "I've got a meeting in fifteen minutes. What's going on? Is everything okay?"

"Everything is fine. Or so I hear." Her eyes flashed, suggesting mischief. "Can't a friend pay a friend a visit without something going on?"

"Normally, a visit from you would be a wonderful thing." Jane turned on the faucet and began washing the accumulation of flour and butter off her hands from the piecrusts she'd just finished making. If Robin was going to pop in for a visit, her timing couldn't have been better since Jane was at a good stopping point. She could spare ten minutes. She really didn't have time to start anything else before the meeting. "But when said visit happens during the lunch crunch, it does make me wonder."

"I get to take a break every now and then." Robin shrugged, trying way too hard to act nonchalant. When Jane arched her brows at her friend, Robin's pretense crumbled like a piece of day-old corn bread.

"You never were a very good actor," Jane said.

"Fair enough." She glanced around the kitchen again and then whispered, "Is it true?"

"Is what true?" Jane whispered back.

Robin made a face and thrust her chin forward as she made a clucking noise. "Jane. You know who I'm talking about." Robin looked around the kitchen again. "The rumors are running rampant out there."

Jane figured that Robin wanted the scoop on Liam, but why was she acting as if royalty was in town?

"That's Savannah for you," Jane said. "One of the hazards of living in a big little town."

"You're messing with me, which means it has to be true that Liam Wright is here—"

Jane feigned surprise and covered her mouth before her hand fluttered to her throat and lingered there as if clutching an imaginary string of pearls.

"He is?" she asked in an exaggerated stage whisper. "Where?"

Robin swatted at the air. "Oh, come on. Gene Knowles said Liam Wright had breakfast with Charles at Clairy's this morning and Charles introduced him as his new business partner.

"So, I have two questions for you. First, why didn't you tell me? And second, why the hell are you pretending like he isn't here? I mean you of all people who used to work for him in New York. You know what this means to Savannah to have a chef of his caliber and notoriety in town."

This time, Jane was the one who glanced around the kitchen. A few minutes ago, Liam had announced the meeting and then had observed a couple of the line cooks, but now he was nowhere in sight. If she knew what was good for her, she needed to get Robin out of the kitchen so that Liam didn't overhear her friend in full fan-girl mode.

Even though she and Robin were close, she hadn't confided the details that had landed her back in Savannah. Robin thought Jane had benevolently left New York to come home and help her mom and Gigi plan and open the tearoom. Until now, Jane had seen no reason to tell anyone other than Ellie otherwise.

With her future at Wila being so uncertain, she didn't want her coworkers dwelling on the fact that she'd previously worked for Liam.

Of course, after the round of introductions, everyone had known, if they hadn't known already. But it hadn't been a topic of conversation. Liam had been in the kitchen a lot since he and Charles had made the announcement yesterday. So the atmosphere hadn't been conducive for her colleagues to try to pump her for information. A couple had tried, but Jane had quickly put a stop to it. The last thing she needed was for Liam to perceive that she was gossiping about him.

The same applied to dishing dirt with Robin while Jane was on the clock.

However, she did get a break, even though she rarely took one.

"Take a walk with me," Jane said to Robin. "Hey, Tilly, I'm going to take a break and step out for a few minutes. I have my cell phone. Give me a ring if you need me."

Her assistant looked at her as if she were speaking a foreign language. *What is this strange word break you speak of?*

"I won't be gone long," she said as she took off

her apron and hung it on a hook near her station. "Will you mix up the peaches for the pie, please?"

Tilly nodded.

"Thanks," Jane said and motioned for Robin to follow her to the back door.

Outside, one of the dishwashers, Jimmy, was sharing a cigarette with one of the newer servers. She was early for her shift. The two, who had been standing a little too close for it to look completely platonic, moved apart. The server—Carol or Karen—was dating another server, who had helped her get the job by lobbying Charles to hire his girlfriend when one of the servers quit without notice. The top buttons of Carol/Karen's white shirt were unbuttoned a little too far to be tasteful. She put one hand on her blouse and took the cigarette from Jimmy with her free hand.

That was some drama waiting to explode if and when the scorned boyfriend caught wind of what was going on. It was always something with the front-of-the-house staff. The kitchen usually ran a little more smoothly.

Liam, she knew, ran a pretty tight ship. In fact, he'd enforced a strict no fraternizing rule at La Bula. As Jane and Robin walked past the couple, Jane wondered how Liam would deal with existing relationships. Maybe he'd turn a blind eye since

Charles hadn't cared. Although, it would be difficult to ignore a love triangle if it got ugly.

It was warm outside. Jane slipped out of her chef's coat and draped it over her arm. In her tank undershirt and cotton pants, she led Robin around the corner, down the alley and out onto the side street that ran perpendicular to Bull Street, the busy street where the restaurant faced.

The sidewalks were crowded with a mix of locals and tourists out enjoying the beautiful sunny Saturday morning. Even though she'd been away for nearly more than eight years, Jane still had an uncanny ability to discern a Savannah resident from a visitor. There was something in the way the locals carried themselves—an unhurried ease with which they moved as opposed to the hungry, eat-it-all-up look that gave away most tourists. She wasn't knocking it. Tourism was good for the local economy. Tourists spent money and ate at restaurants like Wila, and that kept her employed. At least for the next month, she thought as Liam's face popped into her mind.

"Okay, so tell me everything," Robin said. "Is he still as gorgeous in person as he was when you worked for him before? How did he end up here?" She gasped and her eyes flew open wide. "Did he miss you and come here looking for you? That would be too cool."

"No." Jane spat the word like the idea was spoiled and rank. "Absolutely not."

"Good. Then will you introduce me to him?"

Jane rolled her eyes. "Is that why you came all the way over here? To meet Liam Wright?"

Robin smiled and gave a coy one-shoulder shrug.

"Maybe."

Now it made sense. By the time Robin closed the Pig and Whistle in the late afternoon, everyone at Wila would be enmeshed in the busiest part of the day getting ready to open for dinner. Since Robin owned the Pig and it was doing well, she certainly wasn't coming around to ask for a job.

Jane grimaced. "I don't know, Robin. Liam is a little bit…" She racked her brain to think of exactly the right word.

"What? A little bit sexy? A little bit hot? A little bit—"

"No!" Jane snapped, not really wanting to play this game with her friend. She blew out a measured, impatient breath. "Liam Wright is intense. To put it mildly."

"Oooh. I like my men intense. Especially in the bedroom."

"He's not intense that way."

Robin's mouth fell open. "Oh, really? And how

do you know? Are you speaking from personal experience? Do tell, please."

"No. I have not slept with Liam Wright and I don't plan on it, either. He sleeps with models. He doesn't sleep with his employees."

"You're prettier that most models."

Jane waved the compliment away. Not out of modesty, but because...well—

"Not going to happen. In New York, he had a strict no fraternizing policy at La Bula."

"He's the boss, he can do whatever he wants. Rules are meant to be broken. If you had the chance, wouldn't you? I mean, aren't you curious?"

"Okay, there's no denying he's a good-looking guy," Jane said. "If you like tortured, intense, tattooed, authoritarians."

"You'd sleep with him, wouldn't you?" Robin coaxed.

"That's a moot point. Because I'm not his type."

"You're not saying no. I've heard about his penchant for models and actresses. He's had a lot of flings, but that just proves he needs a real woman—someone like you—to capture his heart for real."

"Robin, he's my boss. Stop. It feels highly inappropriate to be having this conversation here."

"Then you owe me a rain check."

Jane grimaced. "That wasn't an invitation for a continuance."

"Not even if I ply you with a couple of martinis before we pick up where we're leaving off?"

Jane scoffed.

"Seriously, don't spoil my fun. This is the coolest thing to happen around here in ages. I wouldn't mind being in the position to have one of Liam Wright's infamous *Breakup Breakfasts*."

"What are you talking about?" Jane asked.

"Haven't you heard about that? There was a story in one of the tabloids about Liam Wright's legendary *Breakup Breakfast*. Apparently, after he's gotten tired of his *flavor du jour*, he fixes this one specific breakfast for her right before he dumps her."

"That sounds charming. It also sounds completely fabricated. How would the tabloid know what he fixes his lovers for breakfast? Much less, his soon-to-be ex-lovers?"

"Apparently, he's been through enough of those model types that they've compared notes and word got out."

Jane laughed. "Are you kidding? What does he fix them for breakfast?"

"Lemon-blueberry crepes. They sounded delicious. I'll have yours if you don't have any plans of having Liam Wright for breakfast."

"Go for it. I usually skip breakfast," Jane said.

"You know what they say, it's the most important meal of the day."

"I'll keep that in mind in case I'm overcome with a sudden craving for lemon-blueberry crepes, but even if they are delicious, I wouldn't be dumb enough to ruin everything by sleeping with my boss."

Obviously, up to that point, the universe didn't hate her enough, because who rounded the corner just as the words *sleeping with my boss* tripped off her tongue? None other than Liam. He stopped and regarded her with a knowing look that wasn't quite a frown. But it certainly wasn't a smile, either.

Robin's mouth fell open then she snapped it shut. She looked so mortified, Jane worried she might melt into a puddle right there on the cobblestone sidewalk. If Jane didn't get hold of herself, she might end up that way, too. She didn't know how much he'd heard.

She shouldn't care what he thought. Even if she did find him attractive, everyone else did, too. And he knew it.

She had no reason whatsoever to be embarrassed. Maybe if she told herself that a couple of hundred times, some of the mortification would subside. Right now, all she could do was fake it until she believed it.

"Hi, chef. This is my friend, Robin Howell. She owns the Pig and Whistle over on Abercorn. Robin, this is Liam Wright, Charles's new business partner."

"Nice to meet you, Robin." His words were brisk. A modified version of the cut direct, but not quite as rude. But it did the job of cauterizing any conversation before it started.

That dark, dark gaze of his held hers for a few beats. "Don't forget we have a meeting in—" He glanced at his watch. His sleeve rode up and she could see the tattoo on his forearm. "Five minutes. Don't be late."

He paused and as the moment steeped in the awkward silence, the corner of his mouth quirked up ever so slightly before he turned and went back the way he'd come.

Chapter Four

*S*leeping with my boss.

Even though Liam wasn't sure of the context in which Jane had said the words, he'd clearly heard her say *sleeping with my boss*.

Now, as he sat at his desk, trying to gather his thoughts for the meeting he'd thought he had all ironed out, he couldn't get her voice out of his head.

He'd just stepped out to go across the street to buy a new phone charger. He'd left his back at the apartment he was renting while in Savannah and needed one he could leave in the office. But he ended up getting a whole lot more than he'd bargained for on that errand.

And he hadn't even gotten his charger. He'd turned around and gone back inside the restaurant without completing the errand.

He thumbed through his legal pad in search of the page where he'd written his notes gleaned during today's interviews.

Sleeping with my boss.

Sleeping with her boss?

Since Charles was old enough to be her grandfather, Liam doubted she was talking about him. That left one boss.

He let the yellow, lined pages fall back into place.

He didn't need notes.

And he'd be an idiot for even thinking about sleeping with Jane Clark.

So why did he keep thinking about it?

Sure, Jane was an attractive woman—with her curves, which had been on full display in that tank top she was wearing. Who knew that's what she'd been hiding underneath that coat? She also had long, silky, brown hair and piercing light eyes.

And a sharp wit and a smart mouth.

He liked it. He liked it all. The entire Jane Clark package.

Hell, who knew?

She was different from the women he usually

found attractive, but there was no denying that this curvy pastry chef had gotten his attention.

And that was a problem. He'd been able to ignore it until now, chalking the attraction up to this different side of Jane that he was only now getting to know.

He tapped his pen on the desk.

They had chemistry.

Yeah, but even though they had chemistry, it didn't mean he had to act on it. In fact, it was up to him to set the tone. And he could do that in the meeting.

Since desserts weren't his strong suit, he was going to have to work closely with Jane. They would be so busy that the last thing she'd think about was *sleeping with the boss*.

In fact, he was going to set such a strong tone, she probably wouldn't like him very much.

He left his office and went to the dining room. The entire crew, minus those who had chosen to leave, was waiting for him. Jane was front and center in that tank top since she hadn't put her jacket back on. He forced himself to not look at her.

"I'll make this quick since we have a lot of work to do before we open tonight," he said. "The individual meetings went well. You've probably heard by now that we lost a few people. It was their choice.

"Anyone who doesn't want to be here is free to go. Those of you who want to stay, know that we have a lot of hard work ahead of us. We'll have a day off tomorrow—Sunday. I'd like everyone to be here on Monday morning at 9:00 a.m. sharp. Bring your A game. We're going to finalize the new menu, which we will start serving when we reopen next week. This week, I will demonstrate each dish that will be on the menu. You will taste everything on the menu and become intimately familiar with every dish.

"I will need to work with pastry—uh, Jane." His gaze locked with hers and he felt that same gut-twisting thrill he'd tried so hard to compartmentalize. He still had some work to do. "Jane, you and I will work together to establish desserts. Desserts aren't my wheelhouse. So, you and I will work closely to develop the dessert menu. Jane, you bring me your best ideas. I'll bring what works at La Bula. Everyone else, come prepared to watch and learn.

"We are going to remake Wila in my image. Does everyone understand that?"

He paused, scanning the faces that were staring back at him, some looking incredulous, as if they'd like to call him an SOB for being such a hard-ass. Silently, he dared anyone to snort, chortle or snicker. It wouldn't have been a good thing. All of them had the sense to realize that. No one so much as cracked a smile. Or so he guessed. He didn't look at Jane.

"Once we reopen, I will be in the kitchen acting as both executive chef and chef du cuisine for the remainder of the month or until I hire replacements.

"Everyone has a month to prove themselves. I'm putting each of you on notice that you should consider the next thirty days a probationary period. I'm giving everyone fair warning that those of you who don't measure up will be let go."

That should be sufficiently unpleasant enough to put Jane Clark off *sleeping with the boss.*

Jane had learned the hard way to expect nothing.

Expectations were a one-way ticket to disappointment.

That's why she'd never expected Liam to give her a second chance.

Expecting something, however, was different from being surprised. The element of surprise, unlike expectation, could be exciting.

Having this second chance compliments of

the man who rarely gave second chances—and to have an entire month to prove herself—was a happy surprise compared to yesterday's gloomy outlook.

Of course, Jane knew the reprieve was thanks to some savvy negotiating on Charles's behalf. And it wasn't just for her. It was for the entire team, but she intended to use this time to show Liam exactly what she could do.

Getting fired had honed her. It had made her stronger—sharper in some ways and calloused in others. While this chance was a surprise, she wouldn't attach too many expectations to it. But she could work damn hard. She would show up every day and do her best work, and she would start tonight.

The kitchen had closed at ten fifteen. It took the staff an hour and a half to clean up and close out. Most of them had been eager to get out and enjoy what was left of Saturday night.

Not Jane. Partying wasn't her gig. Now that the restaurant was quiet, she wanted to use the time to practice a new bread dough recipe she was developing. The kitchen at the Forsyth was small and yummy smells—especially late at night—usually drew guests, even though the kitchen was not a public area.

The lack of a commercial kitchen was one of the challenges they faced when it came to the tearoom.

Jane couldn't make Gigi understand why the health department wouldn't allow them to use the inn's kitchen to prepare food for the tearoom. She kept saying, it worked fine for prepping the guests' continental breakfasts. However, most of the breakfast food was prepackaged or purchased from other commercial kitchens. All they had to do was arrange it on platters and set it out.

They didn't have a place or the funds for adding a new commercial kitchen without doing a major renovation. Ellie's husband, Daniel, who was a professional contractor and had been overseeing the other parts of the remodel at the Forsyth, said it would be even more expensive to bring the current kitchen up to commercial code.

The conundrum made Jane's head hurt and when that happened, she usually sank deeper into her work at Wila.

That's where her mind needed to be anyway.

Liam had told her to be prepared to bake for him. Tasting her desserts was a second interview of sorts.

When she sat down with Liam to discuss the

dessert options for the new menu, she intended to be fully prepared.

She couldn't wait to see the look on his face. He would be the one who was pleasantly surprised.

With today's interview and the staff meeting eating into her time, she'd been so busy she'd only had time to bake the bread and prepare the Saturday dessert offerings.

She needed to take full advantage of this time alone. There was something soothing about being the only one in the kitchen after hours. Even after a thorough cleaning, the place still smelled of the day's deliciousness. It was sort of an olfactory patina built up by years of cooking the same dishes repeatedly.

Jane wondered how the changes Liam wanted to implement would alter the work environment. He'd already shaken things up in the two days he'd been there, she thought as she shrugged out of her chef's coat and pulled up her playlist on her phone. Her favorite songs changed with her mood and tonight she felt like something instrumental, a little romantic and inspiring. Chris Spheeris's *Eros* fit the mood.

As the haunting, sensual acoustic guitar music filled the kitchen, washing away the stress of the day, Jane set out the ingredients she needed for the herb beer bread recipe she would try for the first time: flour, yeast, oil, Parmesan cheese, garlic, an array of spices and, of course, beer.

She went to the pantry, propped open the broken door and took a six-pack of bock, a strong, dark lager, from the shelf. In other recipes, she'd always used a lighter beer and sweeter ingredients. She was eager to see how this darker, savory recipe worked.

Trying a new recipe was always fun. The best part about it was mixing flavors and combinations she'd never tried—again, she never *expected* results. She always gave herself room to make mistakes. She would take notes and try again until she got it right. But she needed that room to experiment and fail and try again until she found her way to the happy surprises.

The search for those surprises kept her busy on a Saturday night. Even though she was never sure how her culinary experiments would turn out, they were a better investment in her time than going out with girlfriends and her sister, Kate, who loved to party and was always looking for romance. Gigi's futile matchmaking attempts had proved that there was no one in Savannah who even remotely interested Jane.

Liam's face popped into her mind unbidden.

She shook her head, as if she could physically fling away the vision. When that didn't work, she blinked for a moment, trying to process her thoughts, trying to put everything into perspective.

She wondered for what had to be the hundredth time how much of her conversation with Robin that Liam had overheard. It shouldn't matter, but Liam was her boss. And he had made it perfectly clear that each and every one of the team was on probation until the end of the month. The deck was already stacked against her because of their history. She didn't want him to get the wrong idea.

She walked over to the sink and washed her hands, scrubbing extra hard, as if she could scrub away the inappropriate thought.

Because she was deluding herself if she thought she was even remotely Liam's type. He liked the tall, leggy, model type. She was short and curvy. While she didn't consider herself unattractive— she never really thought about her looks—her ample curves were a hazard of her job. She loved food way too much to even consider adding *fitting into a size zero*—or even a size six—to her goals.

What was wrong with her? Maybe she needed

a beer to help her relax. It had been a stressful day and a beer did sound good.

She dried her hands, went to the small refrigerator in the pantry and signed out a beer for herself. Reasonable amounts of food and drink were one of the benefits Charles offered the staff. The only thing he asked was that each person record everything he or she consumed in a log that he kept in the pantry. It was an unspoken rule that everyone should "enjoy within reason." The perk wasn't meant to feed entire families, and no one was allowed to remove alcohol from the premises. However, Charles encouraged the staff to share a drink after hours. He said it was good for team building.

Until Liam changed the food benefit, she intended to enjoy.

She sipped the beer and reminded herself that she needed to stop thinking about Liam and focus. She reread the recipe notes she'd jotted down last night. She hyperfocused on weighing out the ingredients for her bread. Where cooking was more of an art that could be forgiving and allowed for margins of variations, baking was chemistry. It was a science that relied on precise measuring, combining and stirring to produce the desired results.

While she set the yeast to proof, she carefully

double-checked the remaining ingredients she'd set out at the ready. They were perfect.

She would mix this batch by hand. She liked to do that with a new recipe. To her, getting her hands in the dough was a more organic approach than letting the mixer have its way with it. Cooking and baking required all the senses—touch, sight, smell, taste and sometimes even the sense of hearing. But tonight, touch was first and foremost on the list.

She used her hands to mix the ingredients in order, taking care not to overmix at this point. Then she turned the sticky dough out onto her floured table, where she began kneading it into a smooth elasticity.

She loved bread. Who didn't love bread? Most models probably didn't, which proved how ridiculous it was for a model and a chef to date. They were polar opposites. The chef's life revolved around food; models didn't eat.

Come on, besides physical attraction, what on earth would a model and a chef have in common?

Most models—except for the rare freak of nature or eating disorder—certainly didn't eat the kind of high-calorie, high-end food on which Liam had built his reputation. Not if they wanted to maintain a sleek, runway-ready body.

Maybe the Breakup Breakfast was actually a test and they'd all failed. All they would've had to do was eat the crepes—and what kind of a person could pass up crepes? Maybe if just one of the models had eaten the crepes, she would've endeared herself and put an end to the Breakup Breakfast curse. Jane was willing to wager that none of them had even tasted a bite.

She could virtually taste the combination of creamy, tangy lemon curd and sweet blueberries. What a bleak existence it would be to live a life without sweets.

"Why do you think they call it the Better Than Sex cake?" she murmured to herself.

Although, something in the fiery glint in Liam's eyes had hinted that sleeping with him would be pretty sweet. Actually, it would probably be more spicy than sweet.

"Spicy sweet," she laughed.

She couldn't help herself. She curled her toes in her black Converse high tops.

Yeah, the model-chef relationship thing…it just didn't make any sense. It had to be the career benefit from the mutual celebrity status that drew Liam to the revolving door of models and actresses.

Well, that and the sex.

That vision of Liam naked in rumpled sheets

flashed in her mind's eye again. Her mouth went dry and she licked her lips. It made her fist her hands into the bread dough, ruining the press-and-stretch rhythm she usually found so therapeutic.

Obviously, it wasn't working tonight anyway.

So, she let her imagination go, led astray by the memory of Ellie's suggestion that a good one-night stand might be the cure for what ailed her. She couldn't seem to stop herself from thinking about Liam in the heat of the act—those sexy, dark eyes, those muscled arms, those tantalizing tattoos. She hadn't even looked close enough to see what they pictured.

But she had noticed that while he wasn't thin, by any means, his body was surprisingly good for a guy whose world revolved around food. He was tall and naturally sturdy…her favorite type of body on a man.

An odd kind of clench-and-release sensation made her belly feel molten-hot and tingle all the way down to her lady parts, which were stretching and yawning as though they were waking up after a deep winter's nap.

That long winter had lasted nearly an entire year after she and Guillermo had broken up—shortly after Liam had fired her. In fact, she'd been out late with Guillermo the night before she'd been fired. He'd complained that he'd felt neglected—further proof that people who didn't work in restaurants didn't understand what taxing, backbreaking work it was. He'd whined, she'd indulged him and had been bone tired when she'd arrived to work her shift the next day—the fateful day that Eduardo Sanchez had paid a surprise visit to La Bula. And the rest was history.

It wasn't really Guillermo's fault. Jane was a big girl and had the power to say yes or no. She'd made her choices and had suffered the consequences. Because of that and the move back to Savannah, it had been a long, dry season.

But sex and one-night stands were the last thing she needed to be thinking about right now. If this was going to work, she could not lose focus every time Liam walked into the room— or popped into her head unbidden. That was unprofessional and a ticket to the express lane to getting fired—again.

She reminded herself that thoughts like this had distracted her the last time she'd made a colossal mistake. And that mistake had cost her her job the first time. Now she had a second chance and she wasn't going to squander it.

She redirected her focus as she gathered the

dough into a ball and punched it down before she started the kneading process all over again, digging the heel of her right hand into the dough, focusing on pressing, stretch and turning. Pressing, stretch and turning. Pressing, stretch and—

Over the music, she thought she heard a noise coming from the vicinity of the back door. She stopped working the bread and muted her music. Maybe it was just the background instruments?

No. There it was again.

She hadn't checked to make sure the back door was locked. She hadn't even thought about it, she'd been so eager to get to work. She'd worked late before, sometimes staying in the Wila kitchen until the wee hours of the morning. There were no windows and the room was walled off from the dining room so that passersby on the street who might look in the windows wouldn't be able to see a light on in the back.

There was the noise again.

This time the sound was unmistakably the back door shutting.

Her heart thudded. She glanced around, looking for a knife or anything she could use to defend herself.

She was grabbing her phone and preparing to

make a run for the front door in the dining room when someone called out, "Hello? Who's here?"

Liam emerged from the hall that led to the back door.

"It's me," she said. "It's Jane."

Liam flinched.

"What are you doing?" she asked. "You scared me to death."

"You scared me, too." He sounded annoyed. "I didn't expect anyone to still be here. Why *are* you here?"

Mild annoyance bit at her, chasing away the lingering traces of fear—and attraction. She gave him a pointed look and gestured to the bread dough on the table.

As Liam started moving her way, she bent into her bread work. The dough was ready to rest and rise. Just to make sure, she gathered it into a ball and tested its elasticity by picking it up and slamming it into the floured marble work surface.

"Remind me not to make you mad," Liam said.

She meant to laugh, but it came out more like a snort.

She infused just enough sweetness into her voice. "Don't say you weren't warned, chef."

His lips twisted into something that resembled

a lopsided smile. For the first time since he'd arrived, he looked almost relaxed.

Almost.

She covered the dough ball in olive oil, put it in a bowl and shielded it with plastic wrap so that it could rise.

Liam peered into the bowl. "What are you working on?"

"A new savory bread recipe I came up with."

"Tell me about it."

"It's a beer bread with a blend of herbs and cheese that I'm in the process of perfecting."

"That's why I smell beer. I thought maybe I'd driven you to drink."

He said the words with a straight face, but Jane gathered this was his attempt at showing that he had a sense of humor.

Two could play that game.

"Apparently, you have." She picked up the bottle, held it up to him in a toast and sipped.

"Mind if I join you?" he said.

"That means you're staying a while?" she asked.

"Unless I'm intruding."

"Of course not. It's your place." She motioned for him to follow her. "Come with me and I'll show you Charles's food and beverage sign-out system."

At the pantry, he stopped at the door and, with one hand holding it open, he motioned for her to go first. If she hadn't been distracted by his good manners, she would've reminded him to make sure the doorstop was in place so the door didn't—

The door slammed shut.

"No!" Jane lunged toward the pantry door, but it was too late.

"Crap," Liam said. "I forgot about the door. But surely there's a way out of here." His hand moved to try the door handle, but in the dim light of the single-bulb fixture, he could see there was no doorknob.

He could also see Jane's stunned face.

Liam took his phone out of his back pocket and switched on the flashlight function to get a better look. There was a borehole where the knob inside the pantry should've been. Liam could see the exposed hardware and the engaged latch mechanism.

He hooked his fingers in the hole and rattled the door, but it didn't give. He tried to turn the latch manually, to no avail.

"Don't waste your time," Jane said. "We're not getting out of here until someone opens the door from the other side. You might want to call someone. Maybe Charles?"

Liam muttered a string of oaths under his breath. "This is crazy. This is a safety hazard. Why would you not fix a broken door that can trap people inside?"

"Are you asking me personally?" Jane's voice was cool but her words were biting. "If you are, you should know that I missed the lesson on replacing door hardware when I was in culinary school. That's why I told you that you needed to be careful."

It had been a long day and he wasn't focused. That's why he'd come back to the restaurant, where he'd planned on soaking up the solitude and ironing out the plan for the new menu. He hadn't planned on running into anyone, much less Jane.

Especially not Jane, after he'd overheard her discussion with her friend.

Now, here they were, trapped together in a spot that was a little cozier than he'd ever intended to find himself in with Jane Clark.

She was still wearing that tank top.

He forced himself to not look at her. Instead, he trained his gaze on his phone.

After switching off the flashlight function, he found Charles's number in his Contacts. He pushed the button to call him—Charles would never let him live this down. That was for sure.

Liam held the phone up to his ear, mentally composing what he was going to say as he waited for the call to go through. But a moment later, nothing happened. The call hadn't gone through.

When Liam looked at the phone screen, it was black. He tapped it. Nothing. Finally, after pressing and holding the button that was supposed to reset the phone didn't work, he realized that his battery was dead.

He had been going at such a hectic pace today, he hadn't found a phone charger after his mission to buy one had been thwarted when he'd encountered Jane and her girlfriend in the alleyway.

He murmured another string of colorful words.

"What's wrong?" Jane asked.

Liam held up his dead phone. "The battery died."

"Are you kidding me?" she said.

"Do you have your phone?" he asked.

"No. My phone is on my workstation. Great. You do realize everyone is off until Monday, right?"

"I was trying not to think about that."

"And this comes from the guy who doesn't give others second chances."

He was stunned silent. At a complete loss for words. She was right, of course. What could he say since he had clearly put his own glass house on full display?

"I'm sorry," she said. "I shouldn't have said that. It was uncalled for."

"No, you're right. I got us into this situation after you had given me due warning. I'll figure some way to get us out of here. There has to be a way out of here."

The last thing he needed was for one of the staffers to come in and find him trapped in the pantry with the pastry chef. That was not a good look or a good tone to set on the first day of training.

He rattled the door again, tried turning the mechanism harder this time, but neither worked.

"Let's chill out for a minute and think about this," Jane said to his back. "Sit down and have a beer."

He turned around and she was standing there holding two beers, one arm outstretched to him as if it was a peace offering.

She really was a good sport. He'd fired her and now he'd gotten the two of them locked in the pantry at the worst possible time. She was offering him a beer and a calm demeanor.

If the situation had been reversed, he would've been a raving lunatic. Why was it suddenly feeling as if Jane Clark was here to teach him a lesson about being a decent human being?

He accepted the beer. "Thanks. And sorry."

She lowered herself onto a large sack of flour and patted the seat next to her.

"Might as well sit here," she said. "Best seat in the house. Or at least the only semi-comfortable one."

Liam hesitated a moment, during which he considered sitting on the hard floor. But even he, who sometimes had a difficult time picking up on subtleties, realized in the nick of time that would look like a jerk move. He joined her on the flour sack.

"Can I ask you a question?" she said.

"Sure." He took a long pull of his beer and waited for her to fire.

"Why do you have such a hard time with people making mistakes?"

"I don't."

"Don't tell me you don't have a hard time with it because you do. It's obvious. That was evident the moment I heard you talking to Bruce. Because I screwed up one time, you were ready to crucify me. Or worse yet, fire me."

Liam shrugged. So now she wanted to talk about this. He had gotten the distinct impression that she was avoiding rehashing what had happened that night at La Bula at all costs.

"Admit it," she said. "If Charles hadn't put the mandate in place that you had to give everyone a chance to prove themselves, you would've let me go without even giving me the benefit of the doubt."

He had been willing to put the issue behind them without discussing it, but if she wanted to reopen it, it was her choice.

"In all fairness, you have to admit you didn't make a simple, run-of-the-mill mistake the night I fired you. You oversalted— Actually, *oversalted* isn't even the word for it. That rum baba tasted like you'd plated a slice of the Dead Sea. And you served it. To a food critic. Why did you do that? Were you trying to ruin me? Because that's what it seemed like from my angle."

"Of course I wasn't trying to ruin you. I nearly ruined my own career. Why would I do something like that on purpose?"

"That's almost as good a question as why you would serve Dead Sea Rum Baba to Eduardo Sanchez. What happened, Jane? I admit I didn't give you a chance to explain yourself that night because I was furious. I was too concerned about trying to keep Sanchez from panning La Bula in *his* magazine. But I'm curious. I'd really like to know. What happened?"

She stared at her hands for a moment then took a long, contemplative drink of her beer before she looked at him.

"Truth?" she asked.

"Always," Liam answered.

"I wasn't the one who made the rum baba recipe that night. It was Kayla—was that her name? She was new and it was my fault for trusting her with the baking that early in the game. And, more than that, it was my fault for not tasting every single batch of cakes she'd mixed up. Based on the way the cake tasted, I figured she had accidentally mixed up the salt and sugar. But I learned that after the fact.

"We were in such a frenzy that night because we were shorthanded. We were totally in the weeds and then, when Sanchez came in, everything went from crazy to uproar."

She shrugged. "In a nutshell, that's what happened. It was the costliest lesson I've ever learned. But you can bet I've never made that mistake again." She pinned him with a pointed look.

"Yet, you took the blame."

"When it all came down to it, it was my fault.

I was Kayla's supervisor. Just as the mistake reflected poorly on La Bula as a whole, not an individual pastry chef or assistant, the mistake in the pastry department was on my head. I had to own it. There was no sense in throwing Kayla under the bus."

Liam laughed. "Oh, so you left me with a pastry assistant who didn't know the difference between salt and sugar. That sounds like the ultimate revenge."

Jane laughed, too. "You know, I never really thought of it that way. Makes me feel a little better."

She had a sense of humor, this one. One thing he'd learned about Jane was that she didn't seem like the vindictive type. However, he had noticed that she had a stubborn streak.

"The only reason I'm bringing this up is that we find ourselves working together again—"

"Oh, does that mean I'm hired?" She smiled and he almost hated to ruin the moment, but he needed to get this out.

"I guess time will tell, but in the meantime, I seem to remember that night at La Bula, I had scheduled another person, but you took it upon yourself to give him the night off. We ended up being short-staffed and that's why we were in the weeds. I hope that won't be a problem *if* we do end up working together again."

Jane's brow knit and then her face softened. "I remember that. And you're right. Jonah Smith, my first assistant, had asked for the night off and I gave it to him. I mean I know Kayla was new, but it was a Tuesday night. I don't know if you remember this, but you had been on me about budget—actually, not me specifically. You'd been after everyone to be conscious of cutting costs. I thought that was a good way to cut back and help Jonah out at the same time."

"I had scheduled him, but you thought you knew better than I did, huh?"

She shrugged and in that instant, he learned something else about her—she was a perfection-ist. She hated to be wrong. Of course, she seemed to think she knew what was best, when experience had proved that wasn't always the case. He had to admit that ballsy streak of hers was sexy—er, attractive—in strictly a boss-employee way.

Sleeping with my boss. Her words echoed in his head and he blinked them away.

"In the future, if it ever comes down to a situa-tion like that, just ask me, okay? In all honesty, it *was* a typical Tuesday night—as far as we knew—before all hell broke loose. If you had asked me if Jonah could've had the night off, I probably would've done the same thing. I would've let him. And, if you had asked me, then the blame would've been on me, not on you. Do we have a deal?"

"Deal." She held up her fist and they bumped to seal the deal.

Her touch slammed into him. Even though it was just a platonic fist bump, he felt a zing when their skin connected. It was probably just the beer. He'd been so busy he hadn't had a chance to eat a full meal. Tasting the various dishes that the staff had cooked up tonight had taken the edge off his hunger. Until now. He was ravenous. That was the only explanation for feeling buzzed after one beer.

He set his bottle down.

"Want another one?" Jane asked.

She was on her feet before he could answer. As she stood, the side of her body brushed against his and her scent lingered. She smelled good—like vanilla and cinnamon and something vaguely floral— even after working such a long day.

"I'll make a deal with you," she said over her shoulder. "I'm saying this because I guess I have nothing to lose. You might fire me at the end of the month, but you might not, and if you don't, at least we will understand each other better. I promise you I will not always approach everything with the attitude that I'm the only one who knows what's best, if you will be more open to giving second chances."

He opened his mouth to say something but she turned around and held up her hand.

"Let me finish, please. If people think they can't make mistakes, you're never going to get the best out of anyone. If you approach it with the attitude of only new mistakes, you'll have the best restaurant in Savannah. I guarantee it. Because the staff will be willing to step outside the box. They will be willing to try new things, and then, if it doesn't work, they know not to make the same mistake again, but to try again and make it better."

As she handed him the beer, her words resonated down to his core. She was sharp. He knew she was right, but it wasn't that easy.

"Point taken. And the bit about you not always thinking you know what's best. Does that apply to your rum baba, too?"

"I wasn't the one who made the Dead Sea Rum Baba," she said.

"That's not the recipe I was talking about."

"Which one? The one you tasted yesterday?"

He nodded.

"What's wrong with my rum baba?" she asked

as she lowered herself back down onto the large sack of flour. "People love my rum baba. In fact, it's the same rum baba I used to fix when I worked at La Bula. You didn't complain about it then."

"Obviously, I never tasted it because you were supposed to be following the La Bula house recipe. But I did taste the batch from last night."

Her face fell. "And? Was there something wrong with it? I noticed that you cleaned your plate. You ate the entire thing. And you left your dish on the end of my table."

He had intended to wash it. He didn't expect the staff to clean up after him. Not even the dish-washers. But he'd gotten busy and by the time he'd returned, the plate was gone.

"It was delicious," he conceded.

"Then why are you bringing it up and acting as if I served you another slice of the Dead Sea cake?"

He laughed. "No, don't get me wrong. This wasn't anything like the Dead Sea version. What I tasted last night was good, but it was…different."

"Different as compared to what?"

"Different from the rum baba I am familiar with. The recipe I know has citrus overtones— both lemon and orange. Yours has something that's

fruity, but it's not citrus. Actually, I couldn't iden-
tify it."

"Apricot glaze." She crossed her arms.

He reached out and touched her.

"Come on, don't be defensive. We both promised to open our minds. All I'm asking is that you
give your recipe a few tweaks this week while
we're working on the dessert menu."

"I'm not pretending to know everything that's
best," Jane said, "but I do know my rum baba.
It's my grandmother's recipe and it is one of the
favorite items on the dessert menu. Actually, it's
one of the bestselling items on the menu, period.
Why would you want to change a good thing? Especially when you've admitted pastry isn't your
wheelhouse."

"It's not, but I know what I like."

She arched a brow at him and something hot
and electric zipped between them.

She looked away and took a drink of her beer.

Liam cleared his throat. "You haven't even tried
my recipe. Will you at least try it?"

She leaned back, resting her head against the
wall. Her arm was flush against his. She didn't
move it, just sat there staring straight ahead.

The skin-on-skin contact set his senses on high
alert. A fire burned in his belly and the tempera-

ture in the small room seemed to increase a few degrees.

She turned her head and looked at him. "Okay. In the spirit of being open-minded—not pretending like I know it all—I will try your recipe. In fact, I have an idea. What if I prepare both recipes for the soft opening at the end of next week and we let the people who attend vote on which one they like best?"

Charles had been working on putting together a guest list for the soft run of their grand reopening. He was inviting friends and family of the staff, local dignitaries and as many of the Who's Who of Savannah luminaries as he could round up on such short notice.

Liam shrugged. When he did, his upper arm slid against hers. "Works for me. But it must be a blind tasting. I don't want you prejudicing anyone. People like you. They don't like me."

"What are you talking about? Women love you." She drawled out the vowels in an exaggerated Southern accent.

Ugh. He wasn't going there.

"I'm saying, the people around here know and love you and your grandmother. That would sway the vote."

She turned her body to face him and smiled at

the idea. "Why, chef, I promise I will do everything in my power to make this fair."

He'd heard traces of her accent before, though he hadn't realized it until now. Maybe it was the beer, but it her words were more relaxed.

"In celebration of my being all open-minded, and giving your clearly inferior recipe a fair shake, I think we should make a wager," she said.

"See, there you go again with your wagers. I think you really are gambler, even if you don't know it."

She playfully backhanded his leg. His thigh burned where she'd touched it.

"I have no idea what you're talking about, I'm sure," she said. "This is just a friendly wager between friends. It shows how proudly I stand behind my rum baba. So, what do you think it should be?"

"I don't know," he said. "Let me think about it."

She was still sitting facing him. The two of them locked gazes and simultaneously narrowed their eyes as if they were trying to come up with the solution to world peace.

He was acutely aware of how her knee was touching his thigh.

He wasn't sure if she was simply comfortable or

if she was buzzed enough to not notice the contact. She was almost finished with her second beer. Actually, it was her third, because she'd had at least part of one before he'd arrived, in addition to the two they'd shared since they'd been locked in. He'd done some damage to his second one, too. It had left him feeling looser and more relaxed than he'd been since he'd arrived in Savannah.

"All right, gambler," he said, "what are you willing to wager—in addition to risking your rum baba's place on the Wila menu?"

She laughed, throwing her head back. The crystalline sound of her voice warmed him from the inside out.

"I don't know. It's not like we'd be competing for a trip to Paris." She slurred her words. "I've never been to Paris. Isn't it crazy that I'm a pastry chef and I've never been to Paris? I've always wanted to go. It's one of my goals," she sighed. "Someday." Her words were wistful and she had a faraway look in her eyes.

"What else is on your list of goals?" he asked.

She looked up at the ceiling, as if recalling it in her mind. "Lots of things. I've only crossed off two things." She leaned in closer and whispered in his ear, "Only two. Isn't that lame?"

"It's better than none." He turned his face toward her and her lips were only a breath away. Suddenly he was the awkward sixteen-year-old, nerd boy, hated by his father and bullied by the cool kids. "So, go to Paris and cross it off your list, too."

She clucked her tongue.

"It's not just a matter of going and crossing it off the list." She made a check mark in the air. "Been there, done that. I want to go and learn the all the secrets of all the great chef pâtissier parisien."

Her French pronunciation was remarkably good for someone whose words were losing their sharp edges and blurring.

"Have you been?" she asked.

He nodded.

"Of course you have. See, I can't go to Paris until I pay off my student loan from culinary school." She picked at the label on the beer bottle and murmured under her breath, "I'm going to be thirty and I'm still paying off student debt." He didn't think she was talking to him until she said, "How long did it take you to get out of debt from school?"

He licked his numb lips so he wouldn't slur, too. "I didn't go to culinary school. I'm self-taught."

She shoved his arm. "Get out! Bad-boy chef, Liam Wright, is self-taught? How did I not know this about you? Though I should've. You're way too cool for school."

He laughed. He couldn't help it. "Bad-boy chef, Liam Wright?" If she only knew. "Is that what you think of me?"

"Honey, that's what everyone thinks of you." The Southern accent that he suspected she consciously controlled was fully slipping now.

In the way, way back of his mind, the part that was shrouded by the beer and the buzz from sitting so close to her, he knew he should be using this time to talk to her about her ideas for the dessert menu. Not about Paris and goals and about why she thought he was a bad boy.

It was front and center in his mind that he'd like to show her that this bad boy wanted to do a lot of things right now, and talking wasn't one of them.

"So, what else don't I know about you?" she asked as she stood. "Where'd you grow up?"

He watched her walk over to the beverage cooler and pull out two more beers.

"Brooklyn."

"Brothers and sisters?" she asked.

"Only child."

"I'm one of three. I can't imagine being an only child. Was it lonely?"

"Sometimes. I guess. I don't know."

"Are your parents still in New York?"

"Dad is. He's a cop."

"Where's your mom?"

"She…um…died when I was fifteen."

"Oh, God, I'm sorry."

She handed him a beer.

"Yeah, me, too. Cancer. It sucks."

"I know. Lost my dad to it when I was young."

"You grew up in Savannah."

"I did. Lived here my entire life until I moved to New York to go to school and work. But we know how that ended."

She gave him a pointed look as she sat next to him.

When she'd settled in, she rested her head on his shoulder.

"I'm sorry about your mom."

"Me, too. I'm sorry about your dad."

"Yeah. It's sad," she said. "Let's not talk about it."

"Okay."

They sat there like that for a while, her head on his shoulder. The beverage cooler ticked. He could smell her shampoo—the floral notes made him want to lean in closer and breathe in deeper.

Suddenly she sat up and turned to him.

"I know!" she said. "If my rum cake wins, you have to take me to Paris."

He laughed. "And if I win?"

"You don't have to take me to Paris."

He chortled. "You're drunk. In what world is that fair?"

She licked her lips and pointed an unsteady finger at him. "It's sorta your fault that I haven't been there yet. If you hadn't fired me, I'd still be in New York. I wouldn't have spent three months looking for a job, running up debt. It set me back. So, you can take me to Paris to make up for it."

Her words were sobering. It stood to reason that losing a job could set a person back, but he'd never thought about it from this perspective. He'd never personalized it and thought about how rash actions could have a devastating effect on someone's life.

It was the alcohol talking—in both of their cases. Her spilling her guts and him feeling bad. But alcohol tended to draw the truth closer to the surface.

"I'm sorry," he said.

"Oooh, don't feel bad." She reached up and stroked his cheek, ran a finger over his lips. The next thing he knew Jane was leaning in and kissing him.

His nerve endings sizzled like live wires under his skin.

And then the whole world disappeared as he pulled her tighter, staking his claim—an unspoken admission of all the things he hadn't allowed himself to think about until now, pouring out in this wordless confession of everything he wanted.

He wanted her.

He wanted her lips—they tasted like hops from the beer, with a hint of chocolate and cinnamon and maybe rum, with just the right amount of salt. Or maybe that was just his imagination, what he'd imagined she'd taste like.

The entire time he'd been in Savannah, since the day he'd seen her sitting in the dining room, his subconscious had craved her kiss.

The logical rational that once had ruled him didn't apply here. Not anymore. Reason shifted and spanned the gap of self-protection until he was thoroughly lost in the taste and feel of her.

Thank God for broken door handles and dreams of Paris and bets about who could make the best damn Dead Sea cake. He wanted to take her to Paris, and to kiss her by the Seine, and to make love to her and wake up with her in his bed. He wanted her. The fact that he was her boss didn't matter.

Except…it did.

The rude, intrusive reality check slammed that fact into focus.

Chapter Five

Oh, God. What had she done?

She'd kissed Liam. That's what she'd done.

The beer was responsible for her indiscretion...
No. *She* was responsible for her indiscretion. The
beer was responsible for her headache.

The horrifying reality of what she'd done was
the reason for her sick stomach.

How could she have been so stupid?

Jane brushed the last uncurled section of her
brown hair before wrapping it around her curling
iron. She grimaced at herself in the mirror, although
her hair was behaving today.

At least something was going right.

She'd leaned in and kissed Liam.

He'd kissed her back—at first. Then, the next thing she knew, he'd pulled away and was determined to free them from the pantry. He'd said it was his fault that they were locked in the pantry and he would get them out. He had. He'd found an old set of cutlery stashed on one of the shelves and had used a table knife to pry the pins out of the hinges and remove the door, freeing them.

If necessity was the mother of invention, then desperation was the force that had propelled Liam to get them out of the pantry. It had been clear that he hadn't wanted to spend another moment in there with her.

As she'd cleaned up her workstation, Liam had apologized and promised it would never happen again. Since he'd left the pantry door leaning against the wall, his meaning was clear: their kiss had been a mistake.

If that's how he felt, she didn't intend to spend her only day off this week agonizing over it.

As she finished putting on her makeup, she decided she would go downstairs and bake the bread she'd started last night at the restaurant but ended up bringing home. By the time they had gotten out of the pantry, it had been too late to fire up the oven.

As if things hadn't been hot enough in the kitchen.

She blinked away the thought—even though she could still feel the phantom tingle of his lips on hers.

The bread—think about the bread, not the kiss.

The extra leavening time had added a new twist to the recipe: the twelve-hour rise. Maybe it would turn out to be one of those happy accidents that made the recipe.

The kiss certainly would never be considered a happy accident. At least the bread gave her hope of something good coming from last night. Suddenly she remembered their bet and their talk about Liam opening his mind and being more patient about new mistakes.

They'd also talked about family. He was an only child who had lost his mom at a tender age. He wasn't quite a child, but he wasn't yet a man. Maybe the loss had created his hard edges?

Sad as it was, it was interesting to glimpse a more vulnerable facet of this complicated man.

She did her best to shake off thoughts of Liam, smoothing her red sundress over her hips and giving herself a once-over in the closet door mirror. She had a standing dinner date with her grandmother, sisters and mother on Monday evenings. Since Jane had Sunday off this week, they'd moved the weekly family meal up a day and decided to have Sunday brunch instead.

When Jane had gotten home, she'd found a note tacked to the door of her bungalow. In the missive, Gigi told her about the change of plans and mentioned that she had a surprise for Jane.

Gigi's "surprises" could be anything from a blind date that she'd arranged for Jane to a croquette recipe she'd decided to try out on the family.

Today, Jane was decidedly hoping for croquettes rather than another croaking frog of a failed fix-up. It had been a while since Gigi had tried to match her up with someone. Jane hoped Gigi wasn't breaking her streak today.

She gave herself one last glance in the mirror, turning first to the left and then to the right. She always tried to look nice for the family meals. Invariably she ended up interacting with the guests or a neighbor would pop in for a quick hello. Dressing up made her feel good. After wearing a uniform of chef's coat and baggy cotton pants five or six days a week, it was fun to reconnect with her feminine side. She enjoyed doing her hair and experimenting with different makeup looks. Today, she'd taken the time to paint her fingernails a cherry red that complimented her dress and pedicure.

Since she had to be at the restaurant so early in the mornings during the work week to start the bread and finalize the daily dessert menu, she rarely had time to bother with extras like makeup and nail polish. Besides, she always kept her fingernails clean, short and unadorned since she had her hands in food every day. There was no place for fussy nail polish in the kitchen. She'd remove her fingernail polish before bed tonight. But her toes were another story. A pedicure was one of the ways she liked to pamper herself after being on her feet all week. Plus, the pedi lasted all week. Even if she was the only one who knew her toes were painted, it was her secret that underneath her high-top tennies, her feet looked pretty.

After sliding on a pair of wedge sandals, which showcased her cherry-red toes, she grabbed the warm beer bread off the kitchen counter and left her bungalow.

She made her way down the shrub-lined pebble path, careful to stay on the larger stepping-stones so she wouldn't step wrong and turn her ankle. As much as she loved pretty heels, her job didn't allow her much practice wearing them since her feet were usually encased in comfy, closed-toed, lace-ups. Ugly shoes were part of her uniform, a hazard of the job that she didn't allow herself to dwell on. She passed the flower garden with its moss-stained angel statue and gurgling fountain and stepped onto the patio area behind the inn.

She had to hand it to her mom, Gigi and Ellie. No matter how much the main building needed repairs or how engrossed Ellie was in the art classes, the women made sure the garden and patio areas were blooming and inviting. They always switched out the flowers to reflect various holidays and made the most of the seasons with tasteful decorations. Often, the Forsyth Galloway Inn was included in Savannah garden tours. Gigi always said it was worth it because it was better publicity than they could buy.

Jane smiled at a man and woman who were lingering over mimosas and a plate of scones at one of the wrought-iron tables on the patio. The sun was peeking through the Spanish moss dripping from trees in Forsyth Park across the street, and the weather was perfect for lingering outside, spending a leisurely morning with someone you loved.

Rather than stealing a kiss when you're locked in a pantry at midnight and having the guy pull the door off the hinges because he couldn't get away fast enough.

Stop thinking about that! Think about some-thing else...

Would she ever have enough time to herself to linger? Would she ever have enough time for love?

She blinked away those thoughts, too, and cast one last wistful smile at the couple as she climbed the stairs that led to the kitchen door. Life was all about choices. She was fully in charge of hers. She chose to work at Wila—and given the circumstances with the change in partnership, she was happy to still have her job—and she chose to devote her free time helping her family plan the tearoom.

She chose to not kiss Liam again.

Jane raised her chin as if daring herself to want anything different. Her family was allowing her to live in the bungalow behind the Forsyth rent-free while she reestablished herself in Savannah. Not only reestablished herself. Because of them, she would be able to dig herself out of the deficit she'd gotten herself into after she'd been fired and had stubbornly decided to stay—much longer than she should've. Really, her family was saving her.

Given the choice of working for someone else or starting her own place at the tearoom at the inn, she'd choose the tearoom. She'd always dreamed of owning her own pâtisserie.

Gigi wanted to start with a tearoom where they offered a basic high tea in addition to other delicacies created by Jane. They were still trying to come up with a viable plan for turning this dream into something profitable enough that it could support a salary for Jane and pay for the remodel.

Jane had done the math. The numbers were distressing. They'd have to sell a lot tea and desserts to pay for the commercial kitchen they needed. Running an ancient bed-and-breakfast, where something was always in need of repair and guest occupancy was erratic, meant money was usually tight. How on earth were they going to pay for it?

In the meantime, Jane was grateful for her job at Wila that paid the bills and happy to spend her spare time dreaming with Gigi. Because what was life without a dream?

When she stepped into the inn's kitchen, Gigi was standing at the stove stirring a steaming pot. She had an apron over one of her best dresses, a yellow floral pattern with a lace collar and cuffs. She was wearing her mother's pearls.

"Good morning," Jane said as she closed the

door behind her. "You look nice. Did you get your hair done this morning?"

Gigi set down her spatula in the spoon holder. When she turned around, she did a double take. "Well, you look extra pretty, yourself." She planted a kiss on Jane's cheek. "Kate came over this morning and washed and set my hair for me." Gigi patted her silver curls.

"Well, you look so pretty, and something smells delicious."

"Thank you, honey. I hope you're hungry. I've been cooking up a feast."

Years ago, Gigi had enrolled in culinary school. A year before she was set to graduate, her mother had passed away unexpectedly, leaving the Forsyth Galloway Inn to Gigi. She'd been so busy managing the inn, she'd never realized her dream of obtaining her culinary arts diploma.

That's why when Jane had showed an interest in cooking, Gigi had been her biggest supporter, teaching her everything she'd gleaned from culinary school and encouraging Jane to follow her dream. While she offered emotional support, Gigi maintained a strict rule of keeping things equal among her three granddaughters. So she'd done what she could to help each of them with school, but the Clark sisters had been responsible for paying for their own post-secondary education.

Jane had never expected a free ride in any area of her life. Only a fair chance.

Her mind flashed to Liam. She hoped he would keep his promise of allowing only new mistakes.

Even if she had initiated it, he'd kissed her back. They both could use a little grace.

"I'm starving," Jane said, turning her focus to the empty table.

Usually, they dined at the trestle table in the kitchen, since it was out of the way of the guests.

"Do you want me to set the table?"

"That would be lovely, honey, thank you," Gigi said as she dried her hands on a white towel embroidered with teacups and a teapot. "We are eating in the dining room today." Without a moment's hesitation, she added, "We're having company join us for brunch. So, add two extra place settings, please."

Jane groaned, not trying to hide her annoyance at the prospect of Gigi's matchmaking. It was difficult to take on a good day, but today, it was the last thing she needed. "Who did you invite?"

A mischievous smile curved her grandmother's lips. "It's a surprise," she said.

Jane slanted Gigi a look. "Is that the surprise you mentioned in the note?"

"Part of it. The guests are a surprise, but that's not *all* the surprise. I think you'll be happy." She sang the last words.

Jane sighed. "What are you up to?"

"Me?" Gigi clutched her pearls and feigned innocence. "What makes you think I would be up to something?"

"Because your reputation precedes you. Maybe I should be more specific. Who did you invite?"

Gigi's brow shot up. "I told you, it's a surprise. You'll just have to wait and see." She turned her back and opened the oven door, checking the biscuits she was baking, clearly signaling the end of the conversation.

Jane realized she was still holding the loaf of bread she'd brought. "Here, I baked this. It's a new recipe I'm trying before I serve it at the restaurant. But since you've made biscuits, you can save it."

"Oooh, looks yummy," Gigi said. "Would it work for the tea sandwiches we want to serve in our tearoom?"

Jane bit back a sassy retort about being a long way from thinking about the menu. Just because she was in a mood, which had darkened at the prospect of having a surprise blind date for brunch when she just wanted to relax and enjoy her family, didn't mean she had to be snippy with her grandmother. Gigi had an unsinkable optimism when it came to the tearoom. It would be mean to skewer her with a reality check. After all, it didn't cost anything to dream.

"Maybe," Jane said as she busied herself gathering plates and silverware. "Which tablecloth and napkins do you want to use?"

Gigi turned around and smiled as she observed what Jane was doing. "The tablecloth is already on the table, darling. So are the good linen napkins. Oh, and let's use the sterling silver today. I've already set out the silver chest. It's on the sideboard in the dining room. While you're at it, use the good crystal champagne flutes and water glasses."

"Champagne flutes? Are we expecting royalty?" Jane asked as she returned the stainless-steel cutlery to the silverware drawer.

Gigi laughed, but she didn't deny it.

"So…you, me, Mom, Ellie and Daniel, Kate and Aidan and Chloe—plus the two mystery guests?" Jane recounted to make sure she had the right number.

Gigi nodded.

Jane took ten china plates out of the cupboard and started toward the dining room, half expecting Gigi to change her mind and insist on using the Royal Doulton china, which they usually saved for only the most special of occasions. But she didn't and Jane pushed through the swinging kitchen door that led to the butler's pantry, which was connected to the dining room.

The doors that separated the private dining room from the lobby area were closed. Jane didn't have to see what was on the lobby side of the doors to know Gigi had put up the sign that read Dining Room Closed for Private Event.

Jane's gaze landed on the elaborate centerpiece of fresh flowers on the formal mahogany dining room table dressed with Gigi's mother's best tablecloth and pressed linen napkins. The silver chest was on the sideboard, exactly where her grandmother had said it would be.

Hmm… Gigi was wearing her pearls. There were fresh flowers on the mahogany table set with her great-grandmother's delicate tablecloth, meticulously pressed linen napkins, their good crystal and sterling silver… Gigi was pulling out all the stops and serving brunch in the private dining room… Add that to Gigi's special hairdo, which meant Kate, who never got up early—especially on her day off—had clearly made a crack-of-dawn house call… Gigi had a standing appointment at

Kate's salon on Thursdays. Sure, there were occasions when Kate had to reschedule…but now that Jane was adding everything up…

Did *Gigi* have a boyfriend? Was he one of the mystery guests?

Jane smiled to herself as she began setting the table. Why else would she have gone to all this trouble getting gussied up on a Sunday morning?

Well, good, she deserved to be happy. And if she had a man to keep her occupied, maybe she wouldn't feel compelled to find dates for her and Kate.

Although, Kate hadn't been on the receiving end of any dates since Jane had returned home because she had recently been involved with Aidan Quindlen, Daniel's brother.

Aidan had been in a motorcycle accident a few months ago and Kate had been looking in on him, helping him shave and cutting his hair for him. Kate, who had never played the good Samaritan, remained rather tight-lipped about her relationship with Aidan, but it showed all the signs of turning romantic.

Of course, Gigi hadn't been trying to fix up Jane lately. Jane hadn't put two and two together until now. Maybe Gigi hadn't stopped the matchmaking because Jane had asked her to. Maybe her grandmother had been otherwise occupied—with a man of her own.

Jane smiled to herself as she placed the final setting and stepped back to look at the pretty table.

That's it. It has to be.

She retraced her steps to the kitchen.

"What's his name?"

"Who's name, honey?" Gigi asked as she tasted the vinaigrette salad dressing she'd prepared.

"What's your boyfriend's name?"

Gigi stopped what she was doing and looked up at Jane.

"Honey, I'm almost eighty-five years old. There's only a man or two out there who could handle me. I'm not sure they're up for the job. I'm too young at heart to get involved with just any old man, but I'm too old for a young man. It doesn't mean I'm closing the door. I'll let you know if and when anything happens."

Jane grimaced as her mind suddenly jumped to the broken pantry door—what it had set in motion and how Liam had all but ripped it off its hinges.

Gigi must've mistaken Jane's look for concern. "I'm absolutely fine with my life. I'm happy and content. That's me in a clamshell. Oh, wait, that's not right, is it? I'm happy as a clam in a nutshell. Or however the saying goes."

Gigi waved her hand in the air. "What I mean is you don't need to worry about me. You, on the other hand, work much too hard. When was the last time you had a date, missy? Hmm?"

I kissed Liam last night.

Jane groaned, audibly. "Gigi, you know the last time I had a date was when you tried to fix me up. And that was a disaster. We've been over and over this subject. I'm too busy to date right now. That's my choice."

"Nonsense." Gigi dismissed Jane's words. "You are in the prime of your dating life, but you work way too hard and too many hours. Do you need me to talk to Charles? I could tell him that you need to get out more and enjoy yourself. Every woman needs a grand romance."

"A grand romance?"

I have to steal kisses in the pantry at work, which is either romantic or mortifying.

Who was she kidding? It was mortifying.

"I mean you should fall in love. You're only young once. You might think all this is going to last forever." She swept her hand up and down, indicating Jane's body. "But take it from somebody who knows. You're on borrowed time. You're almost thirty."

A scoffing noise escaped her throat. "Thanks, Gigi."

The cold, clammy hands of dread suddenly closed around Jane's neck as realization dawned. If this brunch wasn't for Gigi to introduce her new boyfriend to the family, it could only mean one other thing: the mystery guests were for Jane and Kate.

Jane thought about voicing her objections just as she had dozens of times before, or calling Kate and telling her run and save herself, but since Aidan was invited today, Kate was probably safe. Suddenly it felt futile. If the guys were already invited—Jane glanced at the clock—they would arrive within the half hour.

There was no stopping the speeding train that was about to crash into her only day off. She would be cordial. Nothing said she had to see this mystery man again after today. Rather than arguing with her grandmother, which would be like talking to the wall, she would let her actions show Gigi she meant business.

"Oh, that reminds me," Gigi said. "Our birthday is almost here. You'll be thirty. I'll be eighty-five. Let's have a party."

A party? Jane wasn't feeling particularly festive. She made a noncommittal noise and, as she helped Gigi finish the fruit salad and cheese tray, switched the conversation to something more interesting: Gigi's asparagus Fontina quiche recipe.

Everything was ready with twenty minutes to spare.

Gigi said, "Will you be a doll and go out into the lobby to greet our guests in case they arrive early? Your mom and Ellie are out on an early art tour. They should be back by eleven. Daniel should be here soon and Kate is picking up Aidan and Chloe."

"I need to sit down and rest my tired bones for a few minutes before dinner and I don't want—" Gigi stopped midsentence. Her hand flew to her mouth.

Judging by the look on her face, she'd almost let slip the names of the guests. Jane could virtually see the words on the tip of her grandmother's tongue as she mentally reeled them back in.

It was clear that Gigi wasn't going to give up the goods about her plan. Whoever it was would be there soon enough. So, Jane decided to play it cool. She suspected that Gigi got a kick out of watching her squirm almost as much as she enjoyed the thought of finding her a husband. If Jane didn't protest, it might let a little bit of the wind out of Gigi's matchmaking sails.

"Gigi, you go lie down. I will look out for your guests." The older woman didn't protest and Jane's heart tugged a little bit as her grandmother left the kitchen. Gigi equated love and food with happiness and security. Mostly love. But food was a close second. She just wanted Jane to be happy. That's all. Her grandmother was almost eighty-five years old. So she'd let her have her fun today. It wasn't too much to ask. Of course, it didn't mean Jane had to see the guy again. But at least she could lighten up and make her grandmother happy.

Since she had few minutes, Jane made a quick trip back to her bungalow to get her notebook. She might as well get some work done while she waited.

With paper and pen in hand, she went out into the lobby and seated herself at the front desk. First, she straightened the various sightseeing pamphlets and maps from the chamber of commerce that were strewed across the wooden surface—a task that needed tending several times a day after the guests pawed through them. Then she started jotting down notes for a new panna cotta recipe she'd tried but still needed tweaking. She'd just finished writing down her thoughts of how to change the recipe when a group of four women staying at the inn for a girls' weekend approached with questions about Savannah's best ghost tour and fun places to go dancing.

As they left, Jane saw Charles holding the front door for them. Right behind him was *Liam*. Jane's stomach twisted and dropped. *The mystery guests.* She hadn't even considered that Gigi might have invited them, but it made perfect sense—that's why she'd gone to all the trouble to get her hair done and make things so nice.

Even though Gigi would never admit it, she and Charles had been circling each other for years. There was even speculation that he had named the restaurant Wila after her. They'd known each other for decades. The fact that her given name was Wiladean and his restaurant was Wila was too much of a coincidence. Even so, it was the elephant in the room that no one ever dared talk about.

Just as Gigi had sweetly curtailed the earlier conversation when Jane had asked her if she had a boyfriend, she refused to talk about her feelings for Charles, who, no doubt, was the *man or two* who could handle her. Charles was the only man. There hadn't been anyone else since Gigi's husband had passed away decades ago.

Today, however, the bigger elephant would be the kiss she'd shared with Liam last night. Judging from the expression on his face, he looked just as surprised to see her sitting there as she was to see him standing just inside the door of the Forsyth.

She closed her notebook and stood. "Welcome." She mustered her best smile, the one she used for guests of Wila or the Forsyth, on the rare occasion she had to interact with them. Charles leaned in and kissed her on the cheek. Liam kept a safe distance.

He gave her an unreadable look. "What are you doing here?"

Jane bristled. "I live here. What are *you* doing here?"

"I was invited," Liam said. At first, he hadn't recognized Jane, sitting there in that red sundress with her dark hair hanging in loose curls around her bare shoulders. He'd never seen her in anything other than her white chef's coat, baggy drawstring pants and closed-toed shoes. Oh, and that black tank top.

Today, she had tanned legs and red toenails. A frisson of awareness skittered through him, making his eyes open and his palms sweat.

He'd be lying to himself if he tried to convince himself that this was the first time he'd noticed how attractive she was. It hit him that it had started yesterday, when she'd taken off her coat and he'd seen her in that damned black tank top, leaving little doubt that she was all woman.

Somehow, that very obvious fact had escaped him when she'd worked for him in New York. But now, it was clear as…the sexy red polish on the toes at the end of those gorgeous legs. Why? He didn't make a practice of noticing the physical attributes of his employees. Or having brunch at their house—or kissing them in the restaurant pantry, for that matter.

This was awkward. The sudden urge to leave was almost overpowering. But it would be worse if he made up some lame excuse to leave just because he'd suddenly realized that Jane Clark was one hundred percent woman. And a gorgeous woman at that.

"Charles told me his friend Wiladean had invited us to brunch."

"She did," Charles said.

Jane's cheeks flushed pink as she snared Liam's gaze.

"Wiladean is my grandmother. But everyone calls her Gigi."

He wondered if she was thinking about last night. He was. He hadn't been able to get it out of his mind.

"She told me we were having guests, but she didn't mention it was you. But, where are my manners?" Liam was beginning to realize that Jane could flip on Southern charm at will. "Welcome. Please, come in and make yourselves at home."

Jane motioned for them to follow her as she walked through the lobby of the Forsyth Galloway Inn.

Sometimes he would join his employees for a drink after La Bula closed. Drinking with the staff was a restaurant ritual, of sorts. However, after one drink they'd all disperse and do whatever it was they did after hours. Partying. Hooking up. But never with him. He didn't party or hook up with his staff. And he certainly didn't make a habit of kissing his executive pastry chef and then showing up at her home for brunch.

But here he was. Like it or not.

What was it they'd talked about last night?

Only new mistakes. Yeah.

Feeling a little hypocritical, Liam glanced around the lobby and tried to gather his thoughts.

She lived here? In a bed-and-breakfast? That was…different. Although, plenty of people lived in hotels. He guessed… When Charles said they were having brunch at the Forsyth Galloway Inn, he thought they were meeting his friend at a restaurant.

The joke was on him.

The place had a comfortable, lived-in look. Next to the door, a tall, galvanized-metal container held an assortment of umbrellas. It's companion, a leaning coatrack, stood sentry on the opposite side of the door. A grandfather clock ticked rhythmically from the corner. An impressive staircase dominated the center of the room. He half expected to see Scarlett O'Hara looking down on him from the top.

There was a plethora of dark wood, antiques and tchotchkes everywhere—a replica of the Eiffel Tower was perched on an end table next to a merlot-colored wingback chair. On the front desk, a porcelain figurine of a woman in a Southern Belle ball gown held court amid a garden of brochures and pamphlets about things to do in Savannah. Behind that, a collection of teacups and teapots perched on a shelf.

There were several arrangements of artificial flowers—some had seen better days. Several paintings adorned the dark-paneled walls, some depicted floral landscapes, others were of local scenes, such as the famous fountain in Forsyth Park and a streetscape of the historic downtown area. He looked closer and noticed it was Bull Street and the restaurant, Wila, in the lower right corner of the scene.

Suddenly he caught a whiff something delicious. His stomach growled. He hadn't eaten since yesterday. He'd used the morning to catch up on things that had gone by the wayside, such as business at La Bula, which he'd left in the capable hands of his chef du cuisine. He hadn't been able to sleep after he'd gotten back to his apartment. After the sun came up, he'd ventured over to the restaurant, half fearing he'd find Jane there again.

But she hadn't been there. The unexpected pang of disappointment had surprised him.

"My mother, sisters and brother-in-law and a couple of friends will be joining us soon." Jane glanced at her watch and then back at them. Her Southern Belle smile faltered, but only for a moment. "In the meantime, help yourselves to some cheese. What can I get you to drink?

"I have champagne, mimosas, rosé, pinot noir and sauvignon blanc." Jane gesture toward an antique buffet where she'd set out wineglasses, several bottles and an opener. "Or if you'd prefer something stronger, I have bourbon and gin. You could have it on the rocks or I could mix up some Manhattans or martinis."

Maybe he should just have a bottle of Scotch.

And look what happened the last time you had a drink with Jane.

To keep things simple, Liam said, "A glass of red wine sounds fabulous, thanks."

Charles followed suit.

As Jane uncorked the bottle of red, two women and a man entered the dining room.

"There you are," Jane said. Her relief was palpable.

"Gigi invited guests to join us for brunch." Her too wide smile betrayed her, suggesting that she was still as flustered as she'd looked before she'd switched into gracious hostess mode.

"I didn't know we were having guests," said the older of the two women. She looked like the red-headed, green-eyed version of Jane. "But, Charles, it's always good to see you. And who do we have here?"

"Mom," Jane said. "This is Liam Wright. He's my new boss and Charles's new business partner. Liam, this is my mother, Zelda Clark, my sister, Ellie, and her husband, Daniel Quindlen."

If Liam hadn't been looking at that precise moment, he would've missed the exchange of glances between Jane and her sister. But there was no mistaking it. He'd seen it.

Jane caught him looking at her and she immediately turned away and busied herself pouring wine for the newcomers. She handed her sister a glass of club soda. And, again, there was an exchange.

"I'm still trying to wrap my mind around the fact that Charles has taken on a business partner," Zelda said. The statement was general, but she directed it toward Liam.

Liam relayed the abbreviated version of his and Charles's partnership, telling how, for a long time, he'd wanted to open a restaurant in the South and how meeting Charles at the foundation dinner had seemed auspicious.

"Welcome to Savannah, chef," Zelda said. "Don't you hesitate one minute to call on us if you need anything. Charles is like family to us. And I'm sure you're well aware that Wila is one of the best loved restaurants in Savannah. So, don't you go changing it too much." Zelda laughed and her tone was light, but Liam detected a note of unspoken warning in Zelda's voice. "Oh, listen to me. I know Charles wouldn't have brought you into the fold if he didn't have all the faith in the world in you."

He was beginning to notice that people around

here didn't always say what they meant. He was used to a more direct approach. He'd also sensed that some people didn't embrace change very easily. Well, sometimes the stubborn ones needed to experience change as it happened to see the good in it.

Liam flashed his best smile, the one that always managed to win people over, especially in uncomfortable situations. "Thank you for the kind welcome, Zelda. I already love it here."

"You are very welcome," she said. "Now, if you'll excuse me, I'm going to go check on Mama and let her know that her guests have arrived. Jane, honey, why don't you give Liam a tour of the Forsyth? Just like Wila has been Charles's life's work, this inn has been in our family for six generations. Jane can tell you all about it."

Jane topped off Liam's glass of merlot. "How's that?" Her question seemed like a peace offering.

"That's great," he said. "So, you come from a long line of innkeepers."

This was first-class avoidance. He should bring up last night.

Jane nodded.

"What made you shy away from the family business?"

"And this question comes from the NYPD cop's

son." She laughed and he appreciated that she was sparring with him and not making things awkward.

"What makes you think I'm not part of the family business?" She raised a cheeky brow. In this light, her pretty gray-blue eyes looked almost silver.

"My first clue was that you are a pastry chef, not an innkeeper. The second clue was that you work at Wila, not at the inn." He didn't mean to sound so smug.

"Actually, I do work at the Forsyth on my days off."

"You're moonlighting, then?"

"Maybe I wouldn't have to moonlight if I felt like I had more job security."

Pow. It was a direct verbal punch, landed right between the eyes, proving that not everyone in the South took the long way around issues. He appreciated her candor.

"Touché." He nodded and smiled. "I can safely say that barring any repeated mistakes, such as a revival of the Dead Sea cakes, your job at Wila is safe."

She smiled. "Fair enough."

Her eyes searched his for a moment and she looked like she wanted to say something else. But she didn't.

"The staff obviously respects you. A lot. What kind of a businessperson would I be to not recognize that?"

"A pretty bad one."

He laughed. "Well, there you go. I've come to realize I always know where I stand with you. I like that. And, I fully intend to try your *only new mistakes* way of thinking."

"Good to know," she said. She glanced down for a moment then met his gaze again. "Does that mean we're good? I mean, you know…with everything…in the pantry. Even though it's broken, it can be fixed."

She'd emphasized the word *fixed*. Her retreat into ambiguous Savannah-speak threw him. He had to run her words through his mental decoder.

Obviously, she was speaking metaphorically. Not about the lock on the pantry door or how he'd taken it off its hinges to get them out of there.

She was talking about what had happened between them last night.

For a moment, he realized it probably seemed like he couldn't wait to get out of there…away from her. That hadn't been the case. Not at all. That's why it had been even more important for him to get them out of that pantry.

He'd wanted to kiss her again.

Hell, he wanted to kiss her now.

And that was only the start of what he wanted to do with her.

If he had waited for someone to come in and rescue them, who knows what else would've happened. If one of the kitchen staff had found them in there…he hadn't wanted Jane to feel compromised, to have her coworkers look at her as if she was giving special favors to get special favors, when in reality, she was a talented chef and had already proved herself worthy of keeping her post.

He knew the situation was bad if he was worried about what others thought. Beyond food critic reviews, he never worried about opinions.

Until now.

"No worries," he said. "It was my fault for letting the door close. As far as I'm concerned, it's as good as fixed. I hope you do, too."

"Only new mistakes, right?" she said. Her smile didn't quite reach her eyes.

It wasn't a mistake.

"Maybe we should leave the door off the hinges," he said. "That way things can be a bit more…open."

She blinked. Her brow furrowed just the tiniest bit, as if she was trying to translate what that jumble of words meant.

He raked a hand through his hair. Crap, he didn't even know what it meant…except that he couldn't bring himself to say that the kiss they'd shared was a mistake.

But he didn't want to lead her on…because it shouldn't happen again…not at long as she worked in his kitchen.

Still, he couldn't promise himself that it wouldn't happen again.

"I was thinking about what you said last night," he said.

She grimaced. "Um…what did I say?"

"The Dead Sea cake challenge and Paris."

"Oh?" She narrowed her eyes then they flashed. "Oh! What about it?"

"I accept your challenge. We will each prepare our rum baba recipes and have the guests vote on them at the grand reopening at the end of the week. Whoever gets the most votes will have their recipe featured on Wila's new menu. I have to go to Paris next month anyway. If you win, I'll take you with me and introduce you to the best pâtis-siers parisiens."

Her mouth fell open. "Are you serious?"

"Why would I offer if I wasn't serious? You're

right, any pastry chef worth her salt needs to go to Paris. It will only help Wila. It's a win-win."

"If it's a win-win, you must think I'm going to win."

"Not so fast. If I win, for the duration of the probationary month, you have to personally mentor two members of the kitchen staff who don't seem to be on the right track to stay on unless they change their ways."

"Jasper and Joseph?" she asked.

He nodded.

"Yeah, that's not a surprise. But they're good guys at heart. I hope you'll give them a chance."

"Maybe you'll get a chance to help them see the error of their ways."

"I'd love to help, but I'll be in Paris. So, you'd better sharpen your mentoring skills." Her voice teased. So did the playful light in those silver eyes.

Again, something electric passed between them that made Liam take a step back.

"Would you like a tour of the inn?" Jane asked.

"Sure. Is that what you do here? Give tours?"

She scoffed. "No. I'm acting as a consultant for my grandmother and mom. They want to open a tearoom here at the Forsyth. They think I'm their resident expert, their go-to gal for making that happen."

"Aren't you?"

She shrugged. "I guess I am."

And just like that, the rapport between them was easy. She had a talent for making people feel at ease.

"Show me this tearoom?"

She grimaced.

"What's wrong?" he asked.

"We're still trying to nail down the logistics of it."

"Tell me what you have so far," he said. "Maybe I can help."

She frowned. "That sounds like work. I don't want to impose. Not on your only day off."

"You should know by now that I'm a straight-forward kind of guy. I wouldn't offer to help if it was an imposition. In fact, I think it's interesting. Show me where this tearoom will be."

She hesitated for a moment but then crooked her finger in a motion to follow her and he did.

She led him out of the dining room and to a room down the hall. She flipped on a light, re-vealing an empty space that was about the size of a small library or bedroom. It wasn't huge, but it could be adequate. *Maybe.*

"This is the space we have to work with." She crossed her arms in front of her. "I just don't see how we're going to make it work."

Liam shook his head. "I think it could work. What are your reservations?"

She shrugged.

"Maybe I can help. I've never opened a tearoom, but I have a pretty good track record with successful businesses."

She walked him through what she had in mind for the setup.

"My brother-in-law, Daniel, who you just met, is a contractor. He can do the heavy lifting, such as running the water and electric lines from the kitchen and building counter and cabinet space. But we need a commercial kitchen. Where do we put everything? It's not big enough to house even a small commercial kitchen and accommodate more than a handful of guests. Its proximity to the inn's existing kitchen is inconvenient. Even if it was close, the kitchen isn't commercial grade and upgrades are not in budget. Daniel said bringing it to code would cost more than building from scratch."

She turned to him and shrugged.

"Between you and me, I think this is my mom and Gigi's way of keeping me close. Keeping me interested in the inn. It's been in the family for six generations, but my sisters and I have all established ourselves in other careers. Ellie just left her job as an elementary school art teacher to manage the tour and art class amenities we're offering. Actually, the tours and classes are starting to take off. Revenues from that have covered the cost of the first phase of renovations we've done at the inn, but the start-up cost of giving tours and classes is negligible compared to outfitting a commercial kitchen. So, long story short, I'm not holding my breath that the tearoom will ever be more than just a dream."

The late-morning sun was streaming in through the window, casting her in a golden glow, picking out the auburn strands in her brown hair. For a moment, he was struck by her sheer natural, unconventional beauty…but when it came down to it, this woman was smart. She had a no-BS way of looking at the world, and a way of knowing when to call him on his own BS and when to let it slide.

All the women in his past had treated him like the second coming. While being worshipped was initially flattering, it got old fast. Especially when he realized that beyond the superficial attraction, he and all the pretty faces that had come and gone in his life didn't have anything in common and even less to talk about. Hell, most of the women he'd dated didn't even like food.

Common sense dictated that the last thing he needed was to get involved with her family and start giving them business advice. Against his better judgment, he heard himself saying, "I think this has a lot of possibilities. I'm happy to help you with the business plan, Jane."

Chapter Six

Liam Wright was difficult to read. If he hadn't put the trip to Paris on the table—a trip that would benefit Wila—Jane might have thought he was offering to help with the tearoom so that she would have a place to work if things didn't work out at Wila.

She could read a million things into it.

Most likely he thought a little tearoom at a bed-and-breakfast posed no threat to Wila. She'd said she was consulting, not planning on running the place. However, who did he think was going to bake the scones and petits fours?

Before Jane could sort it out, her sister Kate

appeared in the doorway with Aidan's little girl, Chloe, at her side, clutching the stuffed white cat she called Princess Sweetie Pie. "Gigi is summoning everyone to the dining room. She has an announcement to make."

Kate's gaze lingered on Liam. "Who's this?"

"Kate, this is Liam Wright. Liam is Charles's new business partner and my new boss at Wila."

Kate's eyes widened. "Oh!"

"Liam, this is my sister, Kate, and our little friend, Chloe."

Liam made all the appropriate noises.

"Nice to meet you, Liam," Kate said. Chloe hid behind her and peeked out occasionally. "Are you from Savannah?"

"New York."

"You just moved here?" Kate asked.

"No, I'm only here temporarily. For a month, to get the restaurant switched over to the new format. Then I'm going back to New York."

Kate shot Jane a look. It was probably about the restaurant, but all Jane could think about was that Liam would only be here one month. She'd known he was leaving, but until now it hadn't registered that one month was a very short time.

Then he would be gone.

That would be a good thing. Right?

Her mind replayed Ellie's one-night stand cure-all.

She and Liam had had a one-night kiss. They'd managed to get past that. She knew she should leave *well enough* alone, but the kiss and getting past it didn't feel *well enough*. In fact, despite her morning-after regret, seeing him, talking to him—his generous offer to help with the tearoom business plan and to send her to Paris—made her hunger for more.

Jane led the trio back to the dining room. Kate held Chloe's hand as she peppered Liam with questions. Jane was glad for the chance to gather her thoughts, pulling her mind out of the stew of emotions that had begun to simmer. It was a recipe for disaster. She knew it.

"If you need a haircut while you're here, come in and see me," Kate said. "My salon is over on Broughton. It's within walking distance of Wila. Of course, everything that matters is within walking distance of Wila. I hope you're not going to change the restaurant too much. You might end up with a public riot on your hands."

Jane fully intended to pull Gigi aside to ask her why she thought inviting Liam—her boss—to brunch would be a fun surprise. But when she stepped into the dining room, Zelda was pouring a bottle of good champagne—not the drinkable, moderately priced brand they used for mimosas, but the expensive stuff in the green bottle, with the hand-painted flowers—into the good crystal flutes.

"Ah, there she is," Gigi cried when she spied Jane. "Come here, honey."

Gigi beckoned Jane to stand next to her. She complied.

"Oooh! And you must be Liam."

Gigi walked over, took Liam's hand and offered her cheek for him to kiss. He complied. Gigi took a good look at Liam and then turned her gaze to Jane.

"Mmm-hmm, I had a feeling," she said as she gave Liam's hand a squeeze. "I was thrilled when Charles asked if he could bring you today. I would like to get acquainted with you more, but first I have an announcement to make."

Gigi winked at him. Jane recognized the light in her grandmother's eyes.

"Oh, great."

She thought she'd internalized the sigh, but Kate, who was standing next to Aidan, gave her a knowing look and she knew her sister had heard her. Or maybe she'd read her mind.

As Zelda hurried around the room distributing

champagne, Gigi called everyone to order. "I'm so happy you all could be here today. I have a couple of things to say. First, I wanted to remind y'all that Jane and I celebrate our birthday on the same day. We have decided to throw a little soiree for ourselves, and each and every one of you is invited. You, too, Liam."

We hadn't exactly decided, but—

"I'll be sending out save-the-date cards so you can mark your calendars. Now, for the big news. This will come as a surprise for my girls, too. I've managed to find a silent investor for our tearoom. We now have the funds we need for the commercial kitchen, renovation and start-up costs. The Tearoom at The Forsyth is officially a go!"

An investor? Is she kidding?

Zelda, Ellie and Kate sounded a collective gasp, indicating that this was news to them, too.

Never in the one hundred and twenty-five years of the Forsyth's existence had the family taken on an investor. They just didn't involve people who weren't related.

In fact, a few years ago, they'd had a close call when their mother's second husband sued, trying to claim half the value of the inn as marital property when they divorced. He wasn't successful in getting his hands on what he thought was his share, but he'd left Zelda with a mountain of legal fees. That was part of the reason money for renovation was scarce.

His stunt had inspired Gigi to have a lawyer strengthen the terms of the trust protecting the inn from husbands of future generations from pulling a similar stunt.

How did an investor figure in? A more pressing question was *who* was this investor and why hadn't Gigi included her daughter and granddaughter in the discussions?

These were all questions to ask when she and her mom and sisters were alone with Gigi. While Gigi had been eyeing retirement, she hadn't yet signed the Forsyth over to Zelda, who was next in line. A few months ago, her mother had revealed that running the place wasn't her idea of a dream job. She was especially wary after her ex-husband's lawsuit. She claimed that it proved she had more of a creative spirit and not a business head.

To that point, the art classes and tours, a tearoom, and eventual addition of a spa, had been Zelda's ideas. It was designed to entice Ellie, Jane and Kate, who each had careers as an art teacher, a pastry chef and a salon owner, respectively, to come back to the inn and continue the family legacy.

"The construction of the tearoom, will take a

while, but I'm putting you on notice, Liam, that I'm going to do everything in my power to take this talented girl away from Wila and put her in charge of The Tearoom at The Forsyth. Of course, I need to talk to my granddaughter, but getting her away from the restaurant might not be a bad thing." Gigi waggled her brows. "It might open a new, more personal opportunity for the two of you."

"Jane, when you have a moment, may I have a private word with you, please?" Charles asked. She had just finished cooking the apples for a *tressé aux pommes*, a French pastry featuring apples and Armagnac brandy, for the dessert tasting she was preparing for Liam. It was the first step toward finalizing the dessert menu.

"Perfect timing," she said. "The apples need to cool before I can add them to the pastry. Let me finish up here and I'll be right there."

"Very good," Charles said. "Meet me in my office when you're ready."

Jane had prepared *tressé aux pommes*, which translated to apple braid, so many times, she could almost do it in her sleep. It was the perfect recipe for today because she'd been on autopilot most of the morning as her brain had been rehashing and braiding her newfound truce with Liam with the big announcement Gigi had made yesterday.

Gigi had disappeared after the brunch. Jane had looked for her, but she'd been nowhere to be found. Finally, late last night, when Jane saw a light on in the Forsyth's kitchen, she'd found Gigi there.

The two of them had sat down and Jane had firmly but gently told Gigi she'd wished she would've talked to her before she'd announced the plan to steal her away from Wila. Especially in front of her new boss.

Gigi had simply laughed and pooh-poohed Jane's tender admonishments, assuring her that she hadn't intended for Liam to be there but that Charles had asked if he could bring him since he was new in town and she hadn't had the heart to say no. And my, my, my wasn't Liam a handsome *eligible* young man… "The two of you have great chemistry."

There'd been that matchmaking glint in Gigi's eyes.

But Liam would return to New York in a little less than a month. While he was here, they both would be much too busy for Gigi to pull shenanigans.

Even so, after the brunch and the subsequent conversation with Gigi, Jane had spent a restless night, tossing and turning, thinking about the ins and outs of leaving Wila to be her own boss. Funny, though, the more Jane thought about it, the more she realized this could be her golden opportunity... the chance to open her own pâtisserie.

Leaving a steady job would be risky. But Gigi had assured her they would make it happen... *somehow*. Then again, Gigi and Zelda were prone to flights of fancy. Her mother came about it naturally.

The realist in Jane knew she wasn't leaving Wila until she knew for sure that she could support herself and stick to her financial plan to eliminate her student loan and New York debt.

She had a while to think about it before the tearoom would be open for business and need a full-time baker and manager. Of course, if she didn't come on board, they'd have to hire someone else...

As she worked to get to a stopping point before going to Charles's office, Jane realized Tilly was giving her the side-eye.

"May I help you?" Jane asked.

"*Oooh*, somebody's in trouble," Tilly sang. "Oh, but wait, you're Jane Clark. You never do anything wrong."

Jane glanced toward the pantry door that was

still propped against the wall and bit back the urge to say, *Little do you know.*

In addition to lugging all her tearoom baggage to work, when Jane clocked in, the kitchen had been abuzz with all kinds of speculation and questions about why the pantry door was off the hinges.

Jane had kept her head down and Liam, wearing his stoic business face, had quickly put an end to all the inquiries with an authoritative, "The lock is broken. The door will remain off the hinges until we can get it fixed."

She heard none of the innuendo she thought she'd detected yesterday when he'd said, "Maybe we should leave it off the hinges. That way things can be a bit more…open."

She felt silly for thinking he'd been talking in subtle romantic metaphors.

"I wonder what he wants," Tilly said.

"Who?" Jane's heart raced as her gaze darted around the kitchen in search of Liam, but she didn't see him.

"Charles?" Tilly looked at Jane like she was losing her mind. Clearly, she was. That was the only explanation for everything that had happened since Liam had arrived.

"I guess I'll see soon enough." She set the glass dish of apple compote in an out-of-the-way corner of the pastry station, took off her apron and hung it on a peg.

"I'll be right back, but while I'm gone, could you please start weighing out the ingredients for the chocolate mocha cake? Here's the recipe."

Jane opened her notebook to the correct page and placed it in the center of the table. "If anyone is looking for me, tell them I'm with Charles."

Tilly gave her a quick salute.

When Jane got to Charles's office, she stood on the threshold for a moment. He was on a call, but he motioned her in and indicated for her to sit in the chair across from his desk. She had to relocate a manufacturer's sample of a chef's coat, a stack of cookbooks and an unopened sleeve of foam coffee cups from the chair to a shelf on the adjacent wall to clear a space. By the time she'd finished, Charles had ended the call.

"How are you, my dear?" He leaned back in his desk chair and laced his hands behind his head.

"Fine," Jane said. "Crazy busy, but it's all good."

"Is it?" Charles asked.

Jane wasn't sure if he was talking about Liam taking over the kitchen or Gigi's surprise announcement yesterday.

Charles must have picked up on her confusion. "How is Liam working out?"

That was an equally confusing question because it wasn't as if Liam Wright was a new line cook. What choice did she have but to say, "He's fine."

Very fine. And sexy as hell. Quite an accomplished kisser.

"He's getting everything in order. He seems to know exactly what he wants and how he wants it."

"I don't mean to put you on the spot, Jane. But I trust that you would tell me if anything was uncomfortable."

Jane laughed a humorous laugh. "Charles, you *are* putting me on the spot. Liam is seventy-five percent owner of Wila. It's not my place to judge whether things are uncomfortable. I need to keep my job. So even if he had decided to change this place into a burger joint, I'm not going to complain. Well, as long as the burger joint needs an executive pastry chef."

Charles nodded and Jane felt bad for her sarcasm.

For a moment, she wondered if he was second-guessing his decision to sell such a large share of Wila.

"Are you doing okay?" she asked. "Any regrets on your end?"

The older man smiled then scrubbed a hand over his swimmy blue eyes. He was a good-looking guy—the epitome of debonair Southern gentleman with his salt-and-pepper hair and distinguished air.

He toyed with a paperweight on his desk before looking back at Jane. "Yes and no. I suppose I'm experiencing a small dose of seller's remorse." He exhaled a breath that seemed to carry the weight of the world. "But it will pass. For the longest time, this place has been my life. Wila has been my baby in lieu of children. It's outlasted three marriages and carried me through more hurricanes than I care to count. Although, I must admit, sometimes it was hard to tell the difference between the hurricanes and my ex-wives."

They shared a laugh.

"But as you said, it's all good. I suppose it's human nature to second-guess change. But more important than that, there are some things I want to do and owning a restaurant would not allow me the luxury of taking time."

The way Charles was looking at her, Jane sensed he wanted to elaborate.

"Do you want to travel?" she asked.

"I do, but not necessarily…alone."

"There are lots of good group tours out there. Search the web for group tours. You'd be surprised what you'll find. Really, there's something for everyone."

Charles glanced up at the ceiling and that's when Jane realized he was chuckling softly to himself.

"No, Charles, really, it's good to travel with a group. If I was going abroad on my own, I would."

I'm going to Paris with Liam.

The thought popped into her head. Amid the other *happenings*—the kiss, Gigi's announcement— she'd forgotten about the bet. And Paris.

I'm going to Paris if I win the bet.

I'm going to win that bet.

"Jane, my dear, there really is no other way to say this than to just say it. So, I will just come right out with it. Your blessing is important to me. You've always been like a granddaughter to me."

Jane braced herself because she had no idea what he was about to say. Obviously, it was very important. Was he sick? If he was sick, they would move him into the inn and care for him. He wouldn't have to suffer alone. That was the bad thing about being alone at his age. Who did he have to look after him?

"Charles?" Jane leaned forward. "What is it? Are you okay?"

"Jane, I'm in love with your grandmother. I suppose I've always been in love with her, but the time was never right for either of us. When I finally wised up and realized that restaurant hours do not foster a happy marriage… Well, I realized that Wiladean meant too much to me to ruin our relationship like I had with my first three wives.

"Now that I am stepping back from my duties at Wila, she and I are finally free at the same time. We want to see if we can make things work. In some regard, I feel like I've been waiting for this my entire life. Did you know I named this place for her? Wila—short for Wiladean."

Jane's hand fluttered to her throat. She knew. Everyone knew. Now, maybe Gigi would let them talk about it. Hearing it from Charles was just about the most romantic thing she had ever heard in her life. "Does Gigi know how you feel?"

Charles nodded. "We talked about it yesterday after the brunch."

"So that's where she was. I looked for her and couldn't find her."

Charles's love confession probably accounted for Gigi's giddy mood once Jane had found her. It was a sharp contrast from before the brunch when Gigi had chosen her words carefully and said there was only *a man or two* who could handle her. Now that Charles had filled in the blanks, Jane was willing to wager that "a man or two" really meant Charles in Gigi-speak. She was probably being cautious until she knew that he felt the same way. That's why she'd invited him. And Charles had invited Liam.

Now it all made sense.

"If you're asking for my blessing, of course, you have my blessing, Charles. I want nothing more than for you and Gigi to be happy. You're like family. If you and Gigi can be happy together—all the better."

Charles nodded. "Good. Very good. Now, you actually *will* be my granddaughter. I can't tell you how happy that makes me."

Jane blinked back happy tears. If she and Kate couldn't find the men of their dreams and get married, giving Gigi the eighty-fifth birthday present she wanted, at least Charles could make her happy. She deserved to be that happy and more.

Maybe by the time Jane was eighty-five, she'd find her soul mate.

"There is one other reason I asked you to come in here," Charles said. "I have something for you to think about. Once The Tearoom at The Forsyth is up and running, how would you feel about being the owner and proprietor? I'm not trying to steal you away from Liam and Wila, but Wiladean told me how long you've wanted a shop of your own. And how she'd always wanted to give that to you."

"Charles, we're not in any position to make that happen. Not yet. We'd have to sell a heck of a lot of scones and pastries before we could make it profitable enough to generate the salary I make here. You should know that. You created the executive pastry position for me."

"What if money wasn't an issue? What if I could guarantee your salary until the tearoom was up and running on its own? All I would ask in return is for you to work with your mother and sisters to run the Forsyth so Wiladean feels comfortable enough to retire and travel with me."

"Did Gigi put you up to this?"

Charles raised his brow and cocked his head ever so slightly to the side.

Jane gasped. Suddenly everything snapped into place.

"Charles? Are you Gigi's secret investor?"

It made sense. Charles had the proceeds from the sale of seventy-five percent of Wila. If Charles married Gigi, he would be family. That's the only way Gigi would've taken on a business partner, if she was madly in love with someone who was beyond reproach. That was Charles.

"Have you discussed this with Liam?" Jane asked. "The part about me leaving?"

"No, I wanted to talk to you first."

"What do you think?"

"I know he plans on returning to New York in a few weeks. I wouldn't want to leave him in the lurch. I mean if this was something we decided was viable.

"I understand that this is something you need to think about. Why don't you, Wiladean and I plan a time to sit down and discuss the details?"

"Where's Jane?" Liam asked.

"She's in a meeting with Charles," Tilly said.

He picked up the notebook with the mocha cake recipe Tilly had been using as a guide to measuring ingredients.

Liam had given Jane the mocha cake recipe—a new one they'd started serving at La Bula a couple of months ago. It had become one of their bestselling desserts. This recipe in Jane's notebook was similar, but it wasn't his recipe. This one had more chocolate and more espresso powder—

No, this wasn't right.

"Tilly, where did this recipe come from?"

"Um…" The young woman eyed him warily, as if he'd asked a trick question. "Jane gave it to me?" She had an annoying habit of making all her sentences sound like questions when she talked to him. "That's her notebook?" Tilly said. "It's where she keeps all the recipes we use here?"

Liam started thumbing through the pages, hoping to find the original that he had given Jane, but by the time he reached the back of the notebook, he hadn't found it. However, his eyes did fall on something interesting on the last page. It was titled "Goals."

The first three items—Move to New York City. Graduate from culinary school. Work in an upscale restaurant in New York City—were all neatly lined through.

Beneath those three items was a list of seventeen more. Pay off student loan and debt incurred in New York. Go to Paris. Own my own pâtisserie. Get married. Have at least two kids—

That was as far as he read before someone snatched the book out of his hands.

"What are you doing?" Jane asked, annoyance clipping her voice. She snapped the notebook shut and glared at him.

"I was looking for the mocha cake recipe I sent you."

Her brow was still knit into a tight frown when she opened to the front of the book. "It's right here. There was no need for you to go nosing through my personal notes."

She set the book, which was open to her version of the recipe he'd given her, on the table.

"I didn't realize those pages were personal," he said.

"Sorry?" Tilly squeaked. "It's sort of my fault? I told him that was where you kept all the notes and recipes for us to use in the kitchen?"

Jane's face softened. "It's okay, Tilly." She turned to Liam. "The recipes for this kitchen are in the front." She indicated a divider. "The rest is personal." She waved her hand in the air as if erasing the situation. "I'll move my personal notes to a different notebook."

"Again, I'm sorry," he said. "I did not mean to invade your privacy."

She flushed and he had a feeling she was thinking about the other night. Hell, so was he.

He glanced at the open page. "That's not the recipe I gave you."

"This is the recipe that I refined from the recipe that you gave me," she said. "I made it better."

He didn't want to call her out in front of Tilly. He'd learned the hard way that calling someone out in the middle of the kitchen wasn't the best way to handle a conflict. Only new mistakes. Charles was in the office and the pantry wasn't a good place to take their disagreement...for so many reasons.

"You want to—" he jerked his head toward the door "—step outside for a moment, please?"

She followed him outside into the alleyway and stood there with her arms crossed.

"The last time we were at a standoff was when you let your assistant at La Bula, Jonah Smith, take the night off after I'd scheduled him. We both know how that turned out. You're smart and you're a hell of a pastry chef, but you don't always know what's best, Jane. This recipe—or at least the version I gave you—is a favorite at La Bula."

"This isn't La Bula," she said.

"I don't care," Liam said.

"So, I get no say?" she asked.

"Of course, you get a say."

"Just not right now," she said. "When then? When do I get a say in what I bake? You're questioning my rum baba, which has been a favorite at Wila. You won't even discuss the tweaks I've made to the mocha cake. You haven't even tasted it. We sort of talked about *things* yesterday, but we didn't really. We talked around the issue. I need to know that we're okay."

Liam froze and then instantly melted when he looked into her eyes.

When had he lost his rational mind? The last he remembered seeing it was right before he'd seen her in that black tank top, but it was the taste of her lips that had sent him over the edge. Yesterday, those tanned legs and red toenails had rendered him helpless.

"We are. As far as I'm concerned. I have absolutely no regrets."

Jane blinked. "None?"

"Zero. I hope you don't, either." He reached out and tucked a strand of hair behind her ear. His thumb skimmed her jawline…her bottom lip. All he had to do was lean in and—

The kitchen door opened. They jumped apart as they turned to see one of the line cooks standing frozen in the doorway. He had a package of cigarettes in his hand, no doubt heading for a smoke break. He stopped short of stepping outside, looking at Liam and Jane. "Oops. Sorry. I'll come back later."

"No," they said together, a little too emphatically.

"We're just discussing mocha cake," Jane said as if it was the answer to everything.

"Cool," the cook said. "Carry on. Please."

He closed the door, leaving them alone again.

"Liam, I have to let you know that Gigi has found enough money for me to be full-time at the tearoom…the money is from her secret investor."

"It's Charles, right?"

She grimaced. "Did he, uh… Did he tell you that?"

"No, but it's pretty obvious."

She shrugged, smiled, bobbed her head in a noncommittal way that wasn't quite a nod of affirmation, wasn't quite a shake of denial.

"Are you giving me your notice?" he asked.

"The tearoom won't be open for a while. I could help you find my replacement. I'd even help you train the person."

A million thoughts pinged around Liam's brain. But the one that pushed forward and demanded center stage said, "That means once you leave, you won't work for me anymore."

She nodded and he pulled her in to a kiss that tasted like heaven.

Liam had kissed her. This time there hadn't been a drop of alcohol involved and *he'd* kissed *her*.

Maybe that's exactly what she'd expected him to do. It was definitely what she'd hoped he would do…whether she knew it or not.

But she'd just told him about her plan without even knowing if the tearoom could support her. All for a kiss.

The anxious wave in her stomach suggested that this might be the push out of the nest she needed. Maybe. But first she needed to make sure her grandmother wasn't just dreaming out loud and that Charles had been serious.

Even though Charles was a businessperson who wasn't prone to flights of fancy, she needed to talk to Gigi before she made things final with Liam.

And then, of course, there was Liam.

She steeled herself and firmly resolved that the chance of exploring things with Liam would not have a single bearing on her decision to leave Wila.

He'd made her no promises, other than that he was leaving at the end of the month.

Executive pastry chef jobs were not plentiful. Once she relinquished her position at Wila and helped him hire someone else, she was on her own. The again, by relinquishing her position at Wila, she was giving herself the ultimate promotion— the fulfillment of a dream.

Okay, yes, and maybe a chance at love. Liam had been the first guy in a long time—the first since her breakup with Guillermo—to awaken her senses, to make her sit up and take notice.

Liam Wright of all people. He was so not her type. Those tattoos and that attitude. He was so intense. He scared her a little bit. He thrilled her. What was that saying about every day you should do something that scared you?

Yeah—that.

And she wasn't his type, either. Yet here she stood with the feel of his kiss still on her lips. The taste of him still in her mouth.

Maybe that's why neither of them had found anyone. Until now.

She sent Gigi a quick text to tell her she wanted to stop by the inn when the team broke for lunch.

Gigi: Honey, what is it? Is everything okay?

Jane: Everything's fine. Need to talk about the tearoom.

Gigi: I'll make sandwiches and tea.

"This is an unexpected pleasure," Gigi said, when Jane walked into the inn's kitchen. "I can't remember the last time you and I had lunch, just the two of us. I made your favorite—tuna, cheddar and arugula on whole wheat. The arugula is from the garden."

"This is nice, Gigi. Thank you for doing this on such short notice."

"You know there's nothing I'd rather do. I'm happiest when I'm with my family."

Jane had to be back at the restaurant in fifty minutes and that included the ten minutes it would take her to walk from the inn to downtown. She had no choice but to cut to the chase.

"I wish I had more time, but I can't be late getting back to work. This afternoon, I'm working one-on-one with Liam."

"Oh, that Liam is a good-looking boy." Gigi set two plates piled high with sandwiches and homemade sweet-potato chips on the table. "I don't blame you for wanting to get back."

"Gigi, this isn't about Liam. This is about my career."

Mostly. And Liam's kiss.

Her grandmother placed two glasses of iced tea with lemon rounds and mint sprigs next to the plates and then took her seat across from Jane at the table.

"I'm sorry," Jane said. "I didn't mean to snap at you. I'm just a little anxious about things."

Gigi reached out and put her hand on Jane's. Her joints were gnarled and age spots mottled her skin, but they were beautiful hands that were a testament to how she had never hesitated to drop everything and make tuna sandwiches at a moment's notice or be the first one to roll up her sleeves and dive into hard work at the inn. Jane wanted to think that she'd inherited that trait from her grandmother.

"I needed to double-check that the numbers really do add up and we can support this new tearoom. If so, I'd like to give my notice at Wila so that Liam can find someone to replace me and I can help train her or him before I leave."

"Wait right here," Gigi said.

She returned a moment later with a manila folder.

"I think this is what you need to see."

Gigi took several papers out of the folder and laid them out on the table. One was a balance sheet that projected a loss for the first two years. The second year's loss was half of the first. Gigi slid another sheet of paper containing an explanation of how they would meet Jane's salary via a business loan—Jane suspected it was from Charles—and the inn would absorb the loss. Finally, there was a brief outline of how they could make the tearoom profitable by the third year.

Jane's hands trembled as she read the plan that mapped out a path to make her and Gigi's dreams come true.

"This makes sense," she said. "This could work."

"All we need is an executive pastry chef who is part of this family and is willing to take the responsibility of a start-up."

Jane smiled at her grandmother and blinked back the tears swimming in her eyes. "I know just the person for the job."

Liam was happy that Jane had lingered at her station and knocked on the office door after everyone left.

"Do you have a minute?" she asked.

"Always for you," he said.

She held out a piece of paper.

"What's this?" he asked as he took it.

When he glanced at it, he saw that it was her resignation.

"You really meant it," he said. "Everything else aside—and believe me, there are no regrets—makes me feel like I should try to convince you to stay. But you've made up your mind, haven't you?"

She nodded and sat in the chair across from his desk.

"Like I said, I'm happy to stay until after you find my replacement. And I'll help you train whoever you hire."

"I'll take you up on that. I'm not even going to start looking until after we reopen."

"That's smart," she said, as they made their way to the bar.

"Are you up for a drink?" he asked. "We need to toast your new venture."

"That sounds superb," she said. "But one thing I wanted to say is that I understand that, since I'm giving my notice, the Paris trip is off the table. I will make it there someday. In fact, if you want me to make your rum baba recipe instead of mine for the grand reopening, I will. No need for the vote."

He set two champagne flutes on the bar.

"Are you having bettor's remorse?" he asked as he extracted a bottle of Veuve Clicquot from the cooler, brought it around to the other side of the bar and took a seat next to her. "You afraid you'll lose?"

He shot her his most flirtatious smile as popped the cork.

"I am so *not* afraid of you," she said as she watched him pour the bubbly into a flute.

"Good." He handed her one of the flutes and claimed the other for himself. "You shouldn't be. I promise I won't hurt you."

The two of them clinked glasses and fell into an electrically charged silence.

They made small talk for a while, sharing bits and pieces of themselves. Among other things, he told her about how decidedly uncool he'd been growing up in the coolest city in the world, New York. She gushed about her sisters. He learned that she was the oldest of three. When he guessed that she was the popular homecoming queen, the type who would've never deigned to look at him twice, he learned that all three Clark sisters had been homecoming queens in their respective years.

"But I couldn't wait to get out of Savannah and move to New York. It seemed like the place where any dream you have can come true." She sipped her champagne and said quietly, "Or it can swallow you whole."

"I'm sorry I didn't treat you better when you were there," he said.

She shook her head midsip. "Stop apologizing. It was a formative experience. I can honestly say that it was a growing experience. Not a fun one, but I'm a stronger person because of it."

She crossed her legs and her calf brushed his leg.

He shifted to reestablish the contact.

She didn't shy away.

"I'm glad I got the chance to make it up to you," he said. "Why don't you come to Paris with me anyway?"

"Liam… I wish I could, but I can't go to Paris and let Wila foot the bill knowing that I'm leaving to open my own shop."

"What if I wanted to show you Paris?"

She gazed into her drink for a moment. "I wish I could see Paris through your eyes. Maybe someday that will happen, but not right now."

Something between them sparked and ignited.

He shifted closer. His hand was on her back, caressing her shoulder, sliding down her arm until he was holding her hand… She slid off the bar stool, positioning herself so that she was standing in front of him, between his legs.

His breath was hot on her temple…his lips skimmed her cheekbone… She looked up at him and his eyes were hazy and hooded, and the next thing she knew his lips were on hers.

They stood there like that, holding each other, kissing each other for an endless span. It could've been all night; it could've been a moment. All she knew was that a deep, hungry part of her was disappearing into the shelter of his arms, into a place where only the two of them existed—no models, no restaurants, no critics.

No hiding. No pretending. No denying.

Not secreted away in the pantry; not fueled by beer.

Just her and him.

A man and a woman who wanted each other.

"Do you want to get out of here?" she said.

"Yes. I do."

Chapter Seven

The full moon streamed through the Spanish moss and the cicadas sang in the distance, the soundtrack to a balmy, electric night. Liam slipped his hand in hers and her instinct was to flinch away before anyone saw them, but she caught herself before she did.

He wouldn't be her boss much longer.

Even so, it was nobody's business but theirs.

They walked in silence, hand-in-hand down Bull Street with its brick sidewalks and granite curbs, past the shops and restaurants, through Madison Square, skirting the horse-drawn carriages and trollies giving late-night tours of this town that was so familiar. But somehow, tonight seemed shiny and brand new.

When they got to Monterey Square, Liam put his arms around her and pulled her close.

He ravaged her mouth, giving her a preview of what was in store.

"Do you want to go to my place?" she asked.

"My apartment is just a few streets away from the Forsyth. We might have more privacy there. I love your family, but tonight, I'm not feeling very sociable." He pulled her closer and punctuated the thought with another kiss.

Soon she found herself following him up the moss-stained steps of a pretty Gordon Street row house. They paused while Liam unlocked the lacquered red front door that led to the foyer. Another larger staircase stood sentry to the left.

"I'm in the parlor unit," he said as he unlocked yet another door.

"This is it." He flipped up the light switch inside the door. She stepped inside and glanced around while he turned the dead bolt. A long hallway with hardwood floors and an expensive-looking runner sported several doors. The first one to the right was the bedroom.

Climbing stairs and messing with locks was sobering. It brought her back to reality.

Liam, too, because he looked her square in the eyes and asked, "Are you okay? Is this all right?"

She stretched up on her tiptoes and kissed him, wanting to make sure there was no doubt in his mind exactly how okay it was. He leaned in and closed the rest of the distance between them. Then they fell into a hungry kiss, arms wrapped around each other. His hands trailed down her back to cup her bottom. Her hands were in his hair, impatient and ravenous as they devoured each other.

Finally, she took his hand and led him inside the bedroom.

She unbuttoned and shrugged out of her chef's coat, letting it fall to the floor as she tugged him down onto the king-size bed with its toile bedspread, turned down over soft white cotton sheets. There was a dresser and matching nightstand that held a table lamp, but they didn't turn it on. The bedroom windows fronted Gordon Street. The plantation shutters were closed, but light from the street filtered in through the slats. Liam must've partially closed the bedroom door because only a soft glow emanated from the hallway.

They clung to each other as if their next breaths depended on it, and he slid his hands under her tank top. She reveled in his touch, loving the feel of his big strong hands on her skin.

When he gently flipped her onto her back and she arched under him, showing him what she wanted, he pulled back a little. But his lips were still on hers, his hands were still working their magic on her body. "Do you want a drink or something?"

She reached for his belt buckle and, as she undid it, smiled up at him. "Or something."

"Coming right up."

He pressed his lips to her collarbone, exploring the sensitive ridge, lingering over the hollow between her shoulder and throat. He stopped when he reached the neckline of her blouse.

She made an impatient noise. So he eased it up and over her head so that he could rid them of the first of the barriers that stood between them.

Next, he made short order of getting rid of her bra.

"You're so beautiful," he whispered as he helped her wiggle out of it. He tossed it away, letting it fall to the floor.

She wasn't, really. Her sisters and mother were beauties—Ellie, with her blond hair and delicate features; Kate, who was the one who most resembled their mom with that riot of auburn curls and emerald-green eyes.

Jane's body was a little too curvy, compliments

of her affinity for pastry. Her medium-length brown hair was neither straight nor curly and its color was a little too ordinary. Her eyes were too silvery gray to be blue. On occasion, she'd been told that the contrast of light eyes and dark hair was striking, but like the difference between *surprise* and *expect*, *striking* was not the same as beautiful. No matter what Liam said.

But if anyone had ever made her feel beautiful, he had.

She lay there in just her panties. He sank down beside her, tracing his fingertips along the column of her throat, worshiping her breasts, taking one nipple in his mouth and caressing the other one. Need coursed through her, making her hot and ready. He slid his hand down, gently grazing her stomach with his fingertips. When he reached the top edge of her panties, he slid his fingers beneath the silk to find her center. She gasped as his fingers opened her and slipped inside. A rush of red-hot need spiraled through her and she almost came undone. All it took was his touch to send her over the edge.

She almost tore his shirt, she was so eager to get it out of the way. But as her fingers worked his zipper, she stopped.

"Wait a minute," she said. "I didn't bring anything with me. Um… I'm not on birth control."

"Don't worry." He was breathless. "I have us covered."

A low, happy moan sounded in her throat.

"Of course you do." She caught his lower lip between her teeth and sucked it into her mouth.

"I love a man who comes prepared."

"Yeah? Why don't you show me? Less talk, more action. But first, let me take care of us. They're in the other room."

"While you're at it," she said. "Bring several. It's early. I think we're going to need them."

It had been a long time since a woman had gotten to him like this. Jane had unleashed a want in him that rendered him desperate for something he had never known he needed.

Since that first kiss, he hadn't been able to get her out of his mind. This was exactly how he'd imagined her body would feel. Now, he was greedy for her, needing to know every inch of her, too eager to bury himself deep inside her.

When he came back into the bedroom and saw her lying on the bed, waiting for him, the picture of her sent a rush of need spiraling through him. He couldn't stifle a groan.

He tossed the condoms onto the nightstand and stepped out of his jeans. He left his briefs on to force himself to slow down and savor the moment. His body wanted her now, but first, he wanted to commit every inch of her to memory.

Instead of doing what his body demanded, he lowered himself next to her, pulled her close and buried his face in her hair. He breathed in the scent of her. That delicious smell of flowers—jasmine, maybe—and vanilla and cinnamon. A fragrance that was so intimate and had become so familiar. It hit him in a certain place that rendered him weak.

But not unable to function.

Smoothing a wisp of hair off her forehead, he kissed the place where it had lain, then he searched her eyes, needing to make sure she was still okay with this.

"Make love to me, Liam," she answered before he could even say the words.

He inhaled a shuddering breath. "Your lips drive me crazy. They have since that first night."

He covered her mouth with his and kissed her with urgency as he slid her panties down.

Seeming as impatient as he was, she rid him of the last barrier between them, tossing his briefs away. He picked up a condom from the nightstand and sheathed himself.

He held her so close, he could hear her heart beat. He shut out everything else but that sound and the need that was driving him to the brink of insanity.

She pulled him even closer so that the tip of his hardness pressed into her. He urged her legs apart and, with a deep thrust, buried himself inside her.

A moan escaped his throat and his gaze was locked on hers. He slid his hands beneath her bottom, helping her match his moves in and out of her body until they both exploded together.

He held her close, both of them clinging to each other as the aftershocks of their lovemaking gradually faded. As they lay there together, sweaty and spent, Liam was still reveling in the smoothness of her skin, the passion in her eyes, the way they'd fit together so perfectly.

She took his breath away. What they had right now was pretty damn near perfect.

"Let me get this straight," Ellie said. "You're quitting Wila to run the tearoom full-time and you slept with Liam Wright?"

Jane's heart beat faster at the mention of Liam's name.

"That just about sums up my life right now," Jane said.

She and her sister were sitting in the room that would become The Tearoom at The Forsyth, trying to make sense of blueprints that architect Ian Wilder had dropped off earlier that day while Jane was at work. Ellie had just finished an art tour and had returned her group to the inn. Jane was so happy to see her sister, because she was the only one she could trust with the details of last night. She didn't need Gigi expecting an engagement. She didn't need her mom judging her. She didn't need Kate forgetting she'd made a promise not to tell and letting the cat out of the bag in front of her mom and Gigi—and probably Charles, too.

It was just too soon. Even so, she was dying to talk about it.

The night with Liam had been heavenly, but going back to work this morning had been a challenge. Even though she'd given her notice at Wila, they hadn't yet announced it to her colleagues. Charles was the only one who knew and he'd agreed with Jane and Liam that they should wait to announce it until the grand reopening. Even if everyone knew she was leaving, it would have been unprofessional to give even the slightest hint that anything personal was going on between Liam and her.

All day, Jane had taken extra care to keep her

head down for fear of giving herself away. It was a disconcerting game for both of them to appear so aloof after the combustible passion she and Liam had shared last night.

At work, he'd played his part so well, Jane had started to worry that maybe he considered it a one-nighter, but at the end of the day, after everyone had left, he'd told her how much he'd loved their night together. But right now, since they'd be putting in some long nights and early mornings, they'd agreed to wait to see each other again until after the restaurant had reopened. It was just a few more days.

"I'm so jealous," Ellie said. "You have such a glamorous life. I'm just…getting fat."

"And for a very good cause, may I remind you?"

"I'm not complaining," Ellie said. "We're so happy. Besides, I can live vicariously through you and your exciting life and have the best of both worlds."

Wasn't it funny how people always wanted what they didn't have? Sometimes, Jane would've traded it all—New York, owning her own pâtisserie— to have the love that Ellie and Daniel had found.

If she could have that with Liam, all the better… She blinked away the thought. Even though her heart was primed and ready, she couldn't let herself get too carried away. Baby steps. Speaking of—

"When are you and Daniel telling Gigi about the baby?"

"We're telling her at the birthday party. By that time, I'll be about sixteen weeks along. Since we don't know the baby's sex yet, I bought two baby outfits—one for a girl, one for a boy—and I'm going to wrap them up and let her open them. Don't you think she'll love that as a birthday present? I can't wait to see her face."

Jane held up her hands. "Kate and I might as well not even try to get her anything because she doesn't want anything else except a great-grandchild or maybe a couple of grandsons-in-law."

Ellie slanted her a knowing look and made a suggestive noise.

Jane held up her hands as if to ward off the suggestion. "Nope. I can't give her that."

Not yet.

She blinked. *Maybe not ever.*

She had no idea what this thing was with Liam. He was leaving at the end of the month. She was staying...

"Speaking of...how are things with Kate and Aidan? I still can't quite wrap my mind around the fact that they're a couple. Or are they a couple?"

"You know, it's hard to say with Kate. She's such a free spirit. She was so good about looking in on Aidan while he was at the hospital and she's been watching Chloe when he goes to physical therapy. But now that he's out of the hospital, I worry that the relationship might be getting near the end of its shelf life. Aidan is Daniel's brother. He's such a good guy and he's been through so much. Not only with the accident, but with Chloe's mother. You know she's not around. I hope Kate doesn't break his heart...*again*."

Kate and Aidan had history that stretched back to high school. Jane wasn't sure what had happened because she'd been happily ensconced in culinary school in New York. But they seem to have put the ugliness behind them.

"I don't want to speculate about them," Ellie said. "The most important question is what's going on with you and Liam? I mean are you in love with him?"

Yes.

"Love?" Jane hedged. "Aren't you the one who encouraged me to have a one-night stand? Now you're gunning for love?"

Ellie laughed. "Yeah, I suppose I am. But that was the same night you were breathing smoke and venom over the mention of his name. Was it a one-night stand?"

Was it?

"I don't know," Jane said, suddenly engulfed in vulnerability. "I hope not."

"Good! Does this mean Daniel and I get to re-instate the name Liam to our list of baby names?"

Jane laughed. "Let's keep our facts straight. I never wanted you to take it off the list in the first place."

Ellie made conceding noises.

"All that matters is you're glowing," Ellie said. "You really are. It's been a long time since I've seen you look this happy. That makes me think this was more than a one-nighter and has the potential to be something big."

Jane's stomach twisted. "It's complicated. It's too early to label us. Why do we have to label things like this anyway? Besides, he's going back to New York at the end of the month. I'm staying here. I committed to staying in Savannah before things heated up between us. Well, sort of..."

Ellie's eyes flashed with intrigue and she leaned in. "There's more? What happened? Tell me everything."

Jane took a deep breath and spilled the details of her night in the pantry with Liam.

"I never intended for anything to happen. Honestly, until then, I didn't even realize I had feelings for him."

"So, you do have feelings for him?"

"Like I said, it's complicated. You know me. I'm not one for one-night stands. My heart has to be in it before I can take things this far. But the other side of that equation is that I have no idea how he feels or what's going to happen next. Only time will tell, and until then, I need to protect my heart."

"I'd like to propose a toast." Liam held his glass high and looked out into the sea of faces of those who had gathered for the grand reopening of Wila. Because of the training and the hustle to get the restaurant in shipshape, he hadn't had time to meet many people besides the staff and Jane's family and friend, Robin, who were all in attendance tonight.

He was thrilled that the Who's Who of Savannah was well represented.

But the only person he wanted to see was Jane.

His gaze picked hers out of the crowd that was all turned toward him, waiting expectantly. Because of the week's demands, he hadn't been able to spend much time with her.

She held his gaze and gave him a secret smile.

She'd changed out of her chef's coat and baggy pants into a sleek, blue halter dress that accentuated her curves and brought out the color of her eyes. She looked stunning, and all night, he'd found himself scanning the room for her.

"I would like to express my appreciation to everyone for being here to celebrate with us this evening. I was humbled and honored when Charles agreed to bring me on as a partner at Wila because I know his restaurant has a very special place in Savannah. It was our goal not so much to change it, but to freshen the concept and build on what was already a good thing. I would especially like to thank the team here at Wila for all their hard work. They have moved some major mountains this week. Some people tell me that I can be challenging to work with."

He paused to let the crowd have a laugh. "You're laughing like that was a joke. It's not. Just ask the kitchen staff. No, actually, I'm very easy to get along with when the job is done well. Each one of the staff brought their A-game and proved to be an invaluable part of the team. Thank you. Please give them a round of applause for the delicious food you've enjoyed tonight and put your hands together for the front-of-the-house staff for the great service."

Liam lifted his glass to the chorus of applause, cheers and clinking crystal.

They had served the food buffet-style, so that people could try a little bit of everything and could mix and mingle. The night's offerings ranged from the caprese salad and white asparagus stuffed with local wild mushrooms and bacon, to the risotto Milanese, beef carpaccio and an elevated low-country boil, to an array of Jane's desserts, including her version of the mocha cake.

The setup had allowed Liam to circulate and meet the people Charles had wanted to introduce him to, but it hadn't allowed him any time with Jane.

Their one night together had been an appetizer— an amuse-bouche—and the memory of it had vied for his concentration and left him ravenous for more. Now they were so close to being able to spend time together, he could almost taste it.

When the applause died down, he said, "I have to tell a story on someone tonight. She and I haven't always seen eye-to-eye, but she has taught me a lot since I've been in Savannah. The most important lesson I've learned from Wila's executive pastry chef, Jane Clark—" The crowd interrupted with another exuberant round of applause for her. He waited for them to finish and loved the way her cheeks flushed with the attention focused on her.

"She taught me the art of second chances and drawing the best out of people by allowing them the room to make mistakes. As I said, she and I haven't always seen eye-to-eye, and this fact inspired a challenge. The rum baba challenge. I thought my recipe was better. She was convinced that her recipe was better. You voted and she was right. You loved her rum baba hands down. Jane, I promise, only new mistakes from here on out." The crowd laughed. "Unfortunately, for us, Jane is leaving Wila for an exciting new venture. So, we will have to talk about whether or not she will allow us to feature her rum baba recipe on the Wila dessert menu. We can figure that out later. Because right now, I have a very special surprise for her."

Someone catcalled. The crowd laughed again.

Little do they know.

Or maybe they did. Maybe it was obvious. He didn't care, because he was falling for her. Scratch that. He'd already fallen. It scared him to death, but he was tired of hiding it.

"Charles has known Jane most of her life. I'm going to turn this over to him, since he is the one responsible for this surprise."

There was more applause from the rapt audience

as they turned their collective gaze on Charles. But Liam only had eyes for Jane. The color in her cheeks was high and she was half smiling, half giving him the stink eye as she mouthed, *What's going on? What are you doing?*

Liam walked over and stood next to Jane.

"What in the world is happening right now?" she whispered.

He reached down and gave her hand a quick squeeze. "You'll see."

"Hello, everyone," Charles said. "Thanks so much for being here tonight to celebrate the start of this new era at Wila. I've always believed you're only as strong as the people with whom you surround yourself. Not too long ago, I took a chance and created an executive pastry chef position because Jane Clark had decided to come home to Savannah. She is so talented, I figured I'd better snap her up before someone else did.

"It was a good choice because the industry is noticing her. She's doing such a good job that I decided to nominate her for an Oscar Hurd Foundation Award. It's a prestigious award that celebrates upcoming talent and those in the culinary business who make a difference. Jane, I'm happy to announce that yesterday, I received word that you are a finalist. I am on the board, so I got to see an advance list of the nominees. You will be getting the official word tomorrow. But I thought it would be fun to share the news since your friends and family are all gathered around. Congratulations, my dear. Oh, and mark your calendar. There is a dinner next week in New York City at which the award winner will be announced. Jane, no matter what happens, you are a winner in the eyes of everyone in Savannah and the restaurant industry."

As the crowd erupted into applause, Jane's hands flew to her mouth. Then she turned to Liam and he engulfed her in a hug.

"Congratulations," he said.

"How long have you known about this?" she asked.

"Charles told me yesterday."

"At least I know you have a good poker face. You're coming to New York with me, right?"

When Jane's eyes fluttered open the next morning, the first thing she saw was Liam's handsome face. He propped himself up on his elbow and smiled down at her. With a finger, she traced the tattoo sleeve on his arm. His dark hair was disheveled and sexy, his coffee-colored eyes were hooded with sleep. Jane couldn't remember a time when he'd looked more delicious.

After the party last night, they'd taken a bottle of Veuve Clicquot back to his place and celebrated by making love until they were both spent.

Jane stretched. "Good morning." Her voice was hoarse with sleep. She sat up and kissed him. He pulled her body to his and the feel of his warm, naked skin against hers made her want him all over again, but they only had one day off to rest up before Wila opened to the public on Tuesday, and she had plans for them.

"Want to get out of town?" she asked. "I was thinking it would be fun to go over to Tybee Island and go to the beach today. And there's this great divey place on the way that serves the best low-country boil in the southeast. Last night you introduced Savannah to 'elevated low-country boil.' I thought you might enjoy getting your hands dirty and digging into the basics."

They showered and made the thirty-minute drive out to the beach on Tybee Island to relax and get away from the city.

"I hear Charles and Gigi are going to the awards dinner in New York," Liam said as he rubbed sunscreen on Jane's back. The sun was high in the cloudless blue sky and the gulls serenaded them with a maritime chorus. Thanks to the briny breeze blowing in from the ocean, the temperature was just about perfect.

"They are," Jane said. "As a finalist, I get four tickets to the dinner—in addition to myself. I asked my mom to go, but she's had this tour of Peru booked for months. She offered to cancel, but I told her that would be crazy. I promised to call her after they announce the winner. So, if you know of anyone else we should take, let me know."

"What about your sisters?"

She turned so she was facing him and used a hand to hold back a strand of hair the wind kept whipping into her eyes.

"Are you kidding? I have one ticket left. I will not be responsible for the war that would ensue if I chose one of them over the other. For the sake of family peace, neither of them gets to go."

He frowned. "You can have my ticket. Then you can ask both of them."

She leaned in and planted a kiss on his lips. "Nope. But thank you. If it makes you feel any better, Ellie has art classes scheduled and her tours are booked solid—she'd have to cancel them. And Kate is still looking in on Aidan, and taking care of Chloe when Aidan goes to physical therapy."

Liam nodded. "That's right."

"Besides, I think there's more going on between them and she probably wouldn't want be away from him."

Liam's brow furrowed. "But this is a special occasion. I'm surprised she wouldn't want to be there for you. Your family seems so close."

Jane waved away his words. "I mean if I wanted her to be there, she would be. I have no doubt. And it's not that I don't want her to be there, I guess it's just simpler if it's the four of us—you, me, Gigi and Charles.

"Besides, Gigi is the one who should be there. She was the one who inspired me to go to culinary school. I guess I'm being a little selfish wanting to have her all to myself. In addition to you and Charles, of course. The four of us understand the industry. We know what this means. Not that my sisters wouldn't get it, but it wouldn't mean as much to them."

"The restaurant biz is Gigi's thing?"

"Yeah, she went to culinary school back in the day. She didn't graduate because she had to come back and run the Forsyth, but she's always been so supportive of my choice to go to culinary school. I want to share this experience with her."

She told Liam all about the history of the Forsyth. About how her dad died and about Zelda's disastrous second marriage to Fred, who hadn't cared at all about the Forsyth and had almost destroyed their family's legacy. But he hadn't succeeded. She segued into Gigi and Ellie running it and mentioned her mother's reluctance to take over the reins because she thought she didn't have the business sense after almost losing the place to Fred. However, in reality, that was what had spurred on her idea for the art classes, the tearoom and eventually the spa.

"My mom wasn't keen on running the place by herself, but she as long as she has her daughters there to run the place with her, she believes she can do it. Of course, it also gives her more flexibility to run off to places like Peru when she wants."

Jane laughed and reveled in Liam's smile.

"That's basically my family in a nutshell. We're not super big on personal space. We're always up in each other's business, but we wouldn't have it any other way… Except sometimes. That's why I'm being a little selfish about who I bring to the dinner. If it's just the four of us, it's fewer people to coordinate. You know how that goes. But the cool thing is that my sisters understand and won't take offense."

Liam gave a half shrug. "I understand in theory. It makes sense. I've never had to contend with that since it was just my dad and me after my mom died. He was never very supportive of my decision to be a chef," Liam laughed. "It embarrassed him that his son wanted to cook for a living. To him, that was woman's work."

Jane cringed.

"Sorry," Liam said. "Now you know what I was dealing with. Being a chef wasn't macho enough for a cop's son."

"Macho?" Jane laughed.

Liam held up his hands. "His word, not mine. I believe he also used the words *sissy* and *girly*."

Jane ran a hand up Liam's thigh. "I think you're looking pretty macho and manly in those swim trunks."

Liam leaned in and kissed her.

But Jane couldn't stop thinking about it. Her entire family not only supported her career choice, they celebrated it as part of who she was. Just like she supported what made them happy. It dawned on her that it was a testament to the strength of their relationship that she didn't feel pressured to invite them to New York and they would still be thrilled for her no matter the outcome of the awards.

"Surely, he has to be proud of all your success," Jane said.

Liam shrugged off her words and took a bottle

of water out of the cooler. "Who knows? I haven't talked to him in a long time."

"Didn't he congratulate you after you won *America's Best Chef*? Come on, it was on national television."

Liam snorted and made a low scoffing noise before sipping his water.

"I doubt he watched the show. Reality TV isn't his thing. I wasn't going to call and tell him—" Liam flicked some sand off his arm. His lips were a thin line and the muscle in his jaw twitched.

Finally, he looked up. The way he was squinting suggested it was a reaction to whatever he'd been thinking about more so than the glare of sun off the white sand.

"What is it?" Jane asked.

He shook his head and she was willing to let it go because she didn't want to badger him into confiding in her.

"Have you ever seen the show?" he asked.

"Of course. I haven't missed a season, which means I saw you win."

She smiled, hoping to lighten the mood.

"Do you remember the episode where they surprised us and brought in our families? At that point in the competition most of the chefs had been away from their families for about two months and were missing them. It's supposed to be a treat for the contestants. I think there were five or six of us left."

At first, Jane didn't remember.

"Remember, it was the one where we had to cook with them but they blindfolded us. They had to describe the food items to us and we had to give them directions on how to cook—"

"Oh, right! I remember. Did your dad—?" She stopped midsentence and bit her bottom lip. Of course, his dad hadn't been there. Liam had as much as said so.

As if reading her mind, "Yeah, I don't know if they called him, but they ended up bringing in my sous chef at the time, Will Langford, to stand in as family because good ole Malcom, badass Brooklyn cop, couldn't be bothered."

Malcom. That was his father's name. *Malcom Wright.*

"I guess they invited him and he declined." Liam flicked at a shell. "I have no idea. Frankly, I don't care. Will and I cleaned up on that challenge. I ended up winning an extra ten grand, which I split with Will."

Liam brushed the sand off his hands before raking his fingers through his hair. "Everyone else had family show up to support them—one guy spent five minutes trying to explain to his little brother how to use a can opener to open a can of tomatoes. Meanwhile, Will and I are whipping through the recipe because he'd fixed it more often than I had. I guess it was an unfair advantage, but no one seemed to care. They were all so happy to see their families, they were fine with me walking off with the win and the ten-grand consolation prize."

He made a low grunting sound, picked up a shell and tossed it out toward the water.

Jane's heart broke for him, because it seemed like he would've traded the win and the ten thousand dollars for his dad to recognize that he was a good chef—that he had talent.

"When was the last time you talked to him?" Jane asked.

Liam laughed, but it sounded humorless.

"I don't know. A long time ago." He rubbed a hand over his face and gave his head a quick shake. "I don't even know why I'm telling you this. I guess meeting your family and seeing how close you are made me realize that there's a part of me that wishes for that. But…you know… Oh, well. It is what it is."

He shrugged again.

"Why don't you see him while we're in NY?"

Liam laughed and frowned at the same time.

"Remember, I live in New York. So does he. We live within twelve miles of each other, but we've lived separate lives for the past fifteen years. It's not like a phone call will change anything. Besides, this is your weekend. I don't want to muddy the waters with him."

Jane touched his arm and made an empathetic noise. "Family bonds are more resilient than you might think."

He slanted her a dubious look. "That's assuming there was a bond to start with."

"No, I'm serious, Liam. A lot can change in fifteen years. Maybe your dad doesn't know how to reach out? Maybe he sees you now—you're successful. You're a celebrity. By all accounts, you've made something of yourself. You're kind of a big deal. Don't you think it would be a little intimidating to make the first move?"

He lifted his shoulders in a gesture that wasn't quite a yes but wasn't a no.

"When we're there this weekend, why don't you extend the olive branch?"

He started to object—she could tell by the look on his face—but she silenced him.

"This would be a perfect time to do it. You could tell him you've been in Savannah and you're going back, but you were in town for the weekend and you wanted to say hello while you were there. That way, there's more of an urgency for the two of you to get together—"

"Jane. No. Please stop. This is your weekend. This trip is about you. I do want to work things out with my dad, but I'll have plenty of time to do that when I get back to NYC. Think about it—you don't even want to deal with the drama of organizing your family. And you get along with them. You don't need the burden of lugging around my family baggage. But you make a good point. And, yeah, I do want to talk to him. You know, try to talk things out. Eventually."

"Good. And the sooner the better, because it's important," she said. "If you don't have family, you don't have anything."

"You're right," he said. "I get it."

Jane beamed and sat a little straighter.

He laughed. "You do love being right, don't you?"

"I do." Her smile faded too soon. "You said you'd work on things when you get back to New York."

He nodded.

"That means you're definitely going back?"

"Yes. La Bula's in New York."

She sighed. "I don't want you to leave."

He reached out and tucked a strand of hair behind her ear. "The other side of that coin is that Wila is in Savannah. So that means I'll be back. I'll probably be spending more time in Savannah than NYC because Wila will need me."

Her heart ached at the thought of being without him.

"What if I need you?"

"Yeah, ya do?"

She nodded.

"Good, because I could get used to this."

Chapter Eight

Later that evening after they got back from the beach, Liam spent some time at Jane's place. They lingered in the shower, helping each other wash away the salt and sand from their day at the beach and making love under the rain-showerhead until they ran out of hot water.

The sun and fresh air had relaxed them, but the chemistry that never seemed to turn cold threatened to keep them up all night. Since tomorrow's call-time was early because it was the first day that Wila would open to the public, they'd decided to call it an early night so they both could get their rest. It was already close to nine thirty when Liam kissed her goodbye and walked out into humid night.

That's when Jane realized the depth of her exhaustion. Her body experienced a physical ache at the thought of spending the night without him, but now all she wanted to do was sleep.

She went into the bathroom to brush her teeth and moisturize her sun-bronzed skin. As she brushed her teeth, she gathered up an armload of wet towels off the vanity. Her hand brushed something hard. When she lifted the towels, she saw the trim black-leather case that held Liam's cell phone.

She grabbed it and hurried outside, power-walking across the back courtyard out to the street where she looked for him, to no avail. He'd gotten too much of a head start.

She thought about taking it to him at his apartment, but it was dark outside and she was tired. Surely, by now he'd realized the phone was missing. He hadn't come back to get it. That meant either he didn't need it tonight or he figured they'd see each other in the morning and she'd bring it to work.

That would come soon enough.

When she was back inside her bungalow, she held the phone for a few moments, not quite sure what to do with it. It felt odd to be in possession of something of his that was so personal. And, yes, it dawned on her that she was holding in her hot little hand the modern-day equivalent of his little black book, personal diary and photo album all rolled into one.

But she would never snoop.

Even though she was curious.

After all, he'd dated Tatiana Ross, one of her favorite actresses. What if he had pictures?

And what the hell was she thinking? She would never—*never*—invade his privacy like that. Besides, she didn't want to see pictures of him with other women.

Even thinking about it made her feel a little sick to her stomach.

She marched into the kitchen where she'd left her purse and stashed his phone inside. Then she double-checked the front door, turned off the lights and went into the bedroom to finish getting ready to go to sleep.

The moment her head hit the pillow, she thought she heard something. A ringing sound? Was it his phone? She lifted her head.

Nothing.

Really, it had sounded more like a car horn.

The sound had probably drifted in from outside.

She fluffed the pillow, turned over and closed her eyes.

But what if Liam was trying to call to make sure she had his phone? If his apartment had a landline, he could use it. Maybe he'd called his phone once he got back to the apartment to make sure it wasn't lost.

If she didn't answer, he might worry. And stay up wasting time notifying his carrier to suspend service or lock his phone, only to have to undo everything tomorrow.

She sat up and swung her legs over the side of the bed. She only paused a moment before deciding to retrieve it and leave it on her bedside table— just in case he called.

She padded into the kitchen and fished it out of her purse.

For good measure, she pressed the activation button to see if there was a notice of his call.

Nothing.

The screen flashed a number pad and asked for a passcode.

For some idiotic reason, she felt relieved that the device was locked. She didn't know why. She was not going to search his phone. Her cheeks flamed at the thought.

But her thumb stayed on the activation button

just long enough for the number pad to disappear and the question "How may I assist you?" to pop up on the screen.

It was the phone's automated assistant.

She clicked off the application like it was hot or might read her mind and tell Liam that she'd been curious about the pictures on his phone. That was completely ridiculous and she knew it.

She set the phone on her nightstand and put her head on the pillow, wide awake now.

What would people find on her phone if she lost it? Nothing embarrassing or incriminating, that's for sure. Just a bunch of family photos and the space that they were turning into the tearoom.

Her mind drifted back to their talk about family—how Liam had admitted that a strong family would be nice.

Why is he so ambivalent to call his father?

Her family wasn't every family, of course, but in her experience, she'd learned that sometimes you must swallow your pride and be the first one to reach out.

How could his dad not be proud of him?

Malcom Wright, what's wrong with you? How can you let fifteen years go by without speaking to your son?

She turned over onto her other side and adjusted her pillow, trying to get comfortable.

Maybe this was simply an unfortunate case of two pigheaded men, both afraid to be the one to extend the olive branch.

If she could just get the two of them in a room, she'd make them sit there until they talked it out.

Clearly, they needed a mediator. Someone to bring them together.

She flopped over onto her back and blinked at the ceiling.

The pinpricks of a good idea needled her body. She reached out and felt around on the nightstand until she'd found Liam's phone.

She was just going to try something...just to see if she could—

She pressed and held the activation button until the automated assistant activated.

How may I help you?

The words swam on the screen and a line that looked like a sound wave danced beneath them.

"What is Malcom Wright's home phone number?"

The ten-digit number appeared on the screen.

A week later, Liam arrived in New York City with Jane, Charles and Gigi. The four had decided to fly in a day before the Oscar Hurd Foundation festivities to give them time to relax and spend an evening in New York.

The workaholic in Liam knew he should run by La Bula to check on things, but the realist in him knew that if he did, invariably, something would ensnare him and he would end up spending the evening working rather than with Jane as he'd promised.

Of course, it had crossed his mind to take her to the restaurant with him—they could have drinks and dinner—but he'd quickly axed the idea when he thought of all the questions that would rise at the sight of him out on what was obviously a date with the pastry chef he'd fired.

Doubling down on his vow to not go within five blocks of La Bula, he invited Charles and Gigi to join him and Jane for dinner. They declined in favor of trying to score tickets for a Broadway show. They extended the invitation for Jane and Liam to join them, but the thought of spending the evening alone with Jane was more enticing. He politely declined.

Jane was staying at the Marriott Marquis. So were Gigi and Charles. Liam was staying at his own Upper West Side apartment. He and Jane hadn't yet told anyone that they were...involved.

Otherwise, Liam would've invited Jane to drop the pretense of the hotel room and stay with him.

She probably would anyway. She said she was dying to see the view he had of Central Park. Now that he was back in New York, he realized he was eager to see it, too, eager to sleep in his own bed and the next morning to use his French press to make the coffee that he would enjoy as he took in that Central Park view.

Navigating between Jane's hotel and his apartment made him feel like a teenager sneaking around to see his girlfriend—was that what she was? His girlfriend? Until now—until he'd been faced with the very real possibility of being out with her and running into someone who knew him—he hadn't really needed to label their relationship.

Now that they were in the city, the pressure was on to keep the fact that they were sleeping together a secret from her family—only because she hadn't told them yet. That was his only hesitation. It dawned on him that until she told her family—or was comfortable with others knowing before they did—he needed to keep it from his friends and colleagues in New York City. It wasn't that he didn't want anyone to know; it just seemed like anytime he stepped out with a new woman, he managed to attract paparazzi attention. He was no George

Clooney, but even having dinner with her in the city might open Pandora's box.

He wasn't sure Jane was prepared for it. Even though it had been a long time since he'd felt this way about a woman, he wasn't ready for their relationship to belong to anyone but them.

That's what would happen if a photo of them landed in the tabloids. It could be a juicy story—Jane used to work for him, he'd fired her, she moved to Savannah, he bought into a restaurant in her hometown… It would be best if they didn't take chances.

That meant that he'd have to fix dinner for her at his place.

He left her to freshen up at the hotel while he shopped for their dinner.

He sent a car to pick her up at seven. He would've gone himself, but he needed to get dinner started so that he wouldn't be in the kitchen all night.

It was an easy but elegant supper. The market had the most beautiful heirloom tomatoes. So they were starting with bruschetta. It would be simple and clean—chopped tomatoes mixed with minced garlic and onion, basil and olive oil. Then they would enjoy Parmesan risotto, butter-poached lobster. For dessert, he'd picked up an assortment of Ladurée truffles.

He had everything ready and even had a chance to shower and shave before she arrived.

After the doorman sent her up, Liam greeted her with a glass of pinot noir and a kiss that promised what was to come later.

"Are you staying?" he asked when she'd settled herself on a stool at his kitchen island.

"I brought clothes for tomorrow," she said with a knowing smile.

"Will Gigi worry about you if you're not there?"

She squinted him. "First, I will probably be the last person on Gigi's mind tonight. She looked pretty happy with Charles. Plus, if she did come looking for me, she could probably figure out that I'm with you. And if she needs me, she can always call."

"Fair enough." He swallowed against the uncertain feeling he'd grappled with earlier. Jane didn't seem concerned about anyone finding out about them. Was he making more out of this than he should?

"That reminds me, please tell me you don't have plans tomorrow morning," she said.

"Why? What's up?"

"I have a surprise for you."

There was that smile again.

"A surprise? What is it?"

"If I told you, it wouldn't be a surprise."

He washed and dried his hands. He sat on the stool next to hers, faced her and poured her more wine. They talked about what she should expect tomorrow evening at the awards dinner and how, as much as she hated to admit it, she had butterflies.

"It really doesn't matter if I win, but it would be so nice. I keep telling myself over and over it's a dream come true to be nominated."

"You realize that even being nominated means you can pretty much write your own ticket. If you need help with the tearoom, you will probably be able to get it easier. Then again, when you win—" He shot her a devilish smile. She closed her eyes and smiled. "No, seriously," he said, "if you win, you'll get a nice cash prize. That will go a long way toward the tearoom."

"And Paris," she said.

"And Paris," he said. "Definitely Paris."

She inhaled sharply and closed her eyes again. "Oh! I shouldn't even be thinking about things like that. Not yet. I just need to keep repeating my mantra. 'It's a dream come true to be nominated.'"

She opened her eyes and looked at him. "Changing the subject to something completely different, have you made any headway on hiring a new executive pastry chef at Wila?"

"I haven't. And I'll tell you why." He sipped his wine. "I've been wanting to talk to you about something."

He'd planned on waiting until they got back to Savannah to talk business, but since she'd brought it up, now was as good a time as any.

"What if, in addition to the tearoom, you had a commercial client to whom you supplied all its desserts?"

Jane shook her head. "I don't know. I haven't thought about it. It would depend on who the client is and how much they ordered. It's hard to say without running the numbers. I wouldn't know where to find a client like that without doing some research."

"What if Wila was that client?"

The next day, Liam brought Jane breakfast in bed.

Jane noted with satisfaction that there were no morning-after lemon-blueberry crepes on the menu.

Though it wasn't the first time they'd spent the night together, it was the first time they'd been together in New York, Liam's stomping ground.

She wondered what her former coworkers would think if they could see Liam and her now—

Well, not *now*. As in this minute when they

were stretched out on Liam's heavenly king-size bed, covered only by the downy-soft cotton sheet, leisurely eating a breakfast of bagels with cream cheese and lox from Russ & Daughters, which he'd had delivered earlier, and dark, rich coffee that he'd steeped in his French press, and reading the *New York Times*.

His bedroom had high ceilings and large windows that let in the morning light. They were high enough that they didn't need window treatments for privacy and they allowed the most spectacular view of Central Park.

She set her coffee cup on the nightstand and indulged in a languid full-body stretch.

What would her former coworkers think if they could see how far she and Liam had come since that fateful day when he'd fired her...the last time they were together in New York?

She glanced at her phone, checking the time and to make sure Gigi hadn't called or texted. She hadn't, but it was getting close to nine thirty. She'd arranged a little surprise for him this morning and they still needed to shower and get ready.

She'd mentioned it last night, but said, "Don't forget, I have a surprise for you. We need to be in midtown by ten forty-five."

"Ten forty-five *this morning*?" He lowered the

paper he'd been reading and looked at her, simultaneously edging his leg over hers and hooking his foot around hers, as if securing her in place.

"Yes, *this* morning."

"I have to stop by La Bula," he said. "I need to mediate a problem between some of the staff. I thought I'd drop you off at the hotel and then go in for a bit. That way you can do whatever you need to do to start getting ready for tonight."

She snuggled into him.

"But first the surprise," she said.

He tossed the paper aside and pulled her into his arms.

"I can think of all kinds of ways I'd like to surprise you," he said. "None of them require getting dressed or leaving this bed."

He kissed her and she almost lost herself for a moment, but then she remembered that they still needed to get ready and traffic could be unpredictable.

"Hold that thought," she said. "Right now, we really need to get a move on."

He sighed. "What in the world do you have up your sleeve?"

He picked up her bare arm and began kissing the sensitive inner area.

Oh, boy.

Reluctantly, she wiggled out of his grasp.

"Come on. We can't be late."

"Where are we going?" he asked.

She shook her head and smiled. "You'll know soon enough."

At 10:49 a.m., they were standing in front of a diner that Liam had never heard of. Jane held out a piece of paper and compared the address with the numbers on the building.

"This is it," she said.

"You're taking me to a diner? We've already had breakfast. But if you're hungry—"

"Not hungry, but I'd like some coffee. Let's go in."

He opened the door for her and followed her inside.

The place was empty, except for one person— a bald guy—sitting at a table with a coffee cup at hand, elbows on the table, his head bent over a newspaper.

When the door closed, the guy looked up.

Liam's heart stopped.

"Malcom?" Jane beamed.

His dad nodded, unsmiling, and clumsily got to his feet, locking gazes with Liam.

"What the…?" Liam uttered a string of words under his breath.

For a split second, Malcom Wright looked like a moose caught in headlights.

"I shouldn't have come." He reached for his wallet and pulled out a five and dropped it on the table. "But your girlfriend here seemed to think it would be a good idea for us to talk."

Liam turned to Jane. "You did this?"

The light in her eyes had dimmed a bit. "I did. I thought you and your dad could talk. I thought maybe he could use the extra ticket and come with us to the dinner tonight."

"Well, you thought wrong, Jane." He hadn't meant to yell. It just slipped out. His mouth was open to apologize, but his dad cut him off.

"Don't yell at her. You don't have to be a jackass about it."

"Shut the hell up. You are the last person who should tell anyone not to yell. I spent my entire youth listening to you bellow."

Liam gritted his teeth and fisted his hands, trying to tamp down the anger that was shaking his entire body. He was literally seeing red. He turned to Jane and took care to lower his voice to a slow, clipped whisper.

"You overstepped. I told you I didn't want to do

this. Why do you always think you know what's best despite what others say?"

"I'll leave," Malcom said.

"Don't bother," Liam growled.

He turned and walked away from his father and Jane.

Jane tried to call Liam at least a dozen times, but each time her call went directly to voice mail.

How could she have miscalculated so badly? Since Liam had said he wanted to mend things with his dad and Malcom had been receptive when she'd called, she thought if she could get them in the same room they'd sit down and talk it out. Clearly, she'd overstepped. She wished Liam would give her a chance to apologize, but he wouldn't answer his phone.

She'd already apologized to Malcom, who'd seemed to be taking it in stride. Then she'd walked the six blocks back to the hotel. She was in New York City but she spent the entire afternoon sitting in her Times Square hotel room staring at her phone. At one point she'd even contemplated skipping tonight's award ceremony, but what good would that do except make her look ungrateful for the honor the foundation had bestowed upon her?

It wouldn't change what was already done, but

it did make her realize she needed to stop and think before she forged ahead with a plan that involved someone else. Clearly, her life had reached a new low. When she got home, she needed to do some soul-searching. She needed to somehow make Liam see that she hadn't meant any harm. Panic welled up inside her. Losing a job was one thing, but losing the love of her life… How would she recover from that?

Her phone rang and her heart nearly stopped.

It was Gigi calling to ask about tonight's plan. "You sound nervous, honey," she said. "How about if we go to the spa at the Four Seasons and get massages and get our hair done? Liam can spare you for the rest of the afternoon, can't he?"

Longer than that, apparently.

Jane's heart ached.

"I called and they have appointments available," Gigi continued. "But I need to call them right back."

When Jane didn't immediately answer, Gigi added, "My treat, of course. To celebrate your nomination."

"Gigi, it's so sweet of you to offer, but all I want right now is a long, hot bath and a quick nap. I'll see you and Charles at the table tonight."

"Are you sure?" Gigi sounded disappointed

and Jane hated that, but she knew Gigi too well. If they got together, Gigi would sense something was wrong and would pepper her with questions.

"I'm sure. I'll take a rain check, though." Jane infused as much happiness into her voice as she could muster. "We'll make a day of it when we get back to Savannah."

Four hours later, Jane was sitting at the table in the Marriott ballroom with Gigi and Charles, but no Liam.

Jane made an excuse for him during the salad course, but when the wait staff began clearing the entrée plates and serving coffee and after-dinner drinks, Gigi glanced at her watch.

"Should we call him? The ceremony starts in ten minutes. His steak is cold." She had been guarding his plate like she was secret service on special detail, glancing around the room every couple of minutes, as if she expected to see him.

"Is everything all right, honey?" Gigi asked after Charles had excused himself to say hello to someone at a nearby table.

"Of course." Jane forced her best smile.

"I thought you and Liam had been getting… closer?"

Jane pulled a face.

"I mean you two have been spending a lot of time together."

"Gigi, we have been working hard to reopen Wila. That had required a lot of togetherness."

"I sensed that there was more between you."

By the grace of God, the room lights dimmed and a spotlight directed everyone's attention to center stage.

Charles took his seat and Jane officially gave up on Liam.

Her earlier remorse had dissolved into a slow, boiling anger. This award wasn't just about her. It was about Wila, too. It brought recognition to the restaurant. If not for her, he should at least be here for Charles. It wasn't as if they were going to hash things out at the table in front of Gigi and Charles. If he didn't know her well enough by now to know that she wouldn't cause a scene, then he obviously didn't know her at all. Maybe she had overstepped by calling his father and setting up the surprise meeting, but Liam was overreacting.

The emcee had taken the stage when Liam slipped into the empty seat next to Jane.

"Sorry I'm late. Something came up at the restaurant."

The time wasn't conducive for talking. Otherwise they would've had to talk over the speaker and that would've been rude. But Liam wasn't even looking at her. That was fine. At least he was there.

A half hour later, when they announced Jane as the Rising Star Pastry Chef of the Southeast, Liam clapped and congratulated her with a sound pat on the back, but the same walls and air of disconnect that she'd experienced with him when he'd fired her were firmly in place. While Gigi and Charles hugged her as she stood to walk to the podium, Liam seemed to sink deeper into his seat, arms crossed over his chest, his face unreadable.

He wasn't just in boss mode, it felt as if she didn't even know this remote man sitting next to her.

Well, screw him.

At least he wouldn't get the chance to fire her this time...not from the kitchen, anyway... But it felt like he'd already let her go from his life.

Tears stung her eyes as she made her way to the front of the ballroom. Oh, God, she hadn't even written an acceptance speech. It's not that she hadn't had faith in herself. She'd been too busy worrying about him—about how she was going to make amends for what she'd done.

This was a big deal. Her peers were recognizing her talents.

Liam was right about one thing; this weekend

was about her. Or at least this moment was. He may have decided to withhold his love, but she wasn't going to let him take this moment away from her.

She knew exactly how to fix that.

She climbed the stairs onto the stage and lowered her head to accept the medal that was hanging from a red, white and blue striped grosgrain ribbon. As she stepped up to the podium, she took a moment to look at the silver medallion hanging around her neck. The metal was cold in her shaking hand. An etching of Oscar Hurd's face smiled back at her—but he was upside down.

Right now, everything felt upside down.

"Wow," she said into the microphone. "This is such an honor."

First, she thanked the Oscar Hurd powers for recognizing her and bestowing the honor. Then she thanked Gigi and Charles for their love and encouragement before shifting the focus to where it counted.

"I wouldn't be standing here if not for the guidance of Liam Wright."

She paused so everyone could applaud.

"He trusted me enough to give me my first job as an executive pastry chef at La Bula. Then our paths crossed again at Wila in Savannah.

"Liam is the consummate professional. Not only did he teach me the importance of teamwork, because it really does take a village to make a restaurant successful. He has shown me that if you're going to get anywhere in life, you can't be afraid to go for what you want. Sure, you might make mistakes. You won't get anywhere if you're afraid to try because you're too afraid of getting it wrong. Because no one is perfect. It's by learning through our mistakes that you can soar to new heights…

"Liam, here's to only new mistakes."

Chapter Nine

Liam stayed in New York for the week following the Oscar Hurd awards. The night of the ceremony, La Bula's chef du cuisine had walked out fifteen minutes before they opened the doors for dinner. That's why he'd been late to the awards dinner. He should've texted Jane to let her know why, but he'd been furious over her betrayal. Because that's what ambushing him and expecting him to make up with his dad on the spot like that had amounted to. A betrayal.

Even so, after too many sleepless nights, he'd called his dad and apologized for acting the way he had. To his surprise, his old man had been cordial.

Or at least willing to listen. Because after Liam had thought about it, despite his dad's transgressions of the past, the guy had schlepped all the way to midtown to begin the process of healing their relationship. He'd explained to his father the element of surprise coupled with the impending La Bula crisis made him lose his cool.

Hearing the words coming out of his own mouth had made him realize he was more like his old man than he cared to admit. It had also underscored how hard it was to maintain relationships when you're married to your restaurant. When a crisis happened, everything else took a back seat. Every day seemed to be a new crisis of one kind or another, which was exactly why Charles wanted to lighten his load and live a little before it was too late.

Even so, Charles had agreed to oversee things at the restaurant while Liam was in New York mending things at La Bula. By this point, Liam knew he had to trust his team.

Trust.

He had a hard time with trust. Jane had pointed that out after the awards ceremony. Only, she'd called it *trust issues*. What did she expect when she'd interfered in the situation with his dad? After the dinner, she'd apologized, but before she'd turned around and walked away, she'd said that she thought there was more to his reaction than simply being put off by the element of surprise.

"Clearly, I overstepped and I'm sorry for that," she'd said. "But I think there is more going on here."

"More?"

"I don't want to turn this into something that's all about me. But I think this has something to do with where our relationship is going as much as it has to do with the issues between you and your father. Since we've been back in New York, I sort of feel like I'm your secret, Liam."

"What are you talking about?"

He'd known exactly what she'd been talking about.

He wasn't by any means embarrassed to be seen with her—on the contrary. He certainly wasn't an A-list celebrity, but his dating life had been tabloid fodder. If someone had gotten a picture of them, the paparazzi would be all over it and people with cell phone cameras and social media accounts could be downright mean. He hadn't wanted to put her through that. Savannah was a different story. It was her turf and the chances of someone recognizing him out of context—well, before Wila reopened and word got out that he was involved—it wasn't as likely as in New York.

"You know exactly what I'm talking about," she'd said. "It was cozy living in our bubble, but…"

She'd pulled a face that was regret mixed with hopelessness.

He hadn't known what to say.

She hadn't given him a chance. "I'm starting to put it all together. Until you make amends with your dad and forgive him for however he wronged you—until you work through this injury you're nursing—I don't know that you're going to be able to sustain a relationship with anyone."

Her words had felt like a well-aimed arrow. No one he'd dated in the past had cut to the heart of the matter like she had. With the others, they'd enjoyed themselves and then when it was time to move on…they'd moved on.

This felt different. Jane felt different. Maybe that's why he'd been so hesitant to go public in New York. Or maybe things had just run their natural course and it was time to move on. This was why he dated people outside his industry.

"You're probably right," he'd said. She did love being right. Even when she was wrong. Because obviously she couldn't see how very wrong he was for her. "Maybe we need to give ourselves some space to think about things."

She'd shaken her head. The look on her face had broken his heart.

"That's exactly what I'm talking about," she'd said. "Goodbye, Liam."

The only problem was, even after a week away from her, his heart hadn't been as willing to let go. It had been a long time since a woman had stayed in his system like this when he should've been well into moving on with his life.

But all he could think about was her.

That's why he was nervous about going to Jane and Gigi's birthday party. But he was back in Savannah and Charles had asked him if he was coming.

His stomach tightened at the thought of seeing her.

It would be the first time they'd talked since New York. He did need to know if she was still willing to supply the desserts for Wila. With all the turmoil, he hadn't been able to look for a new executive pastry chef. She was a businesswoman. He knew her well enough to know that she wouldn't want to lose this opportunity.

But he needed to know for sure, because on the off chance that she'd changed her mind, he needed to interview other candidates. That was a task he didn't relish. He couldn't settle for anyone who was less than the very best.

Jane was the very best.

Yet he was letting her get away. But that's the way it had to be right now. He was being pulled in too many different directions to add a relationship into the mix. If he was married to La Bula, Wila was his mistress, which meant there wasn't much of him left for Jane.

She deserved so much more than leftovers.

He'd walked the half mile from his apartment to the Forsyth, carrying two bouquets of flowers and a bottle of champagne. Because what did you get an octogenarian who seemed to have everything?

And how did you break the ice with the woman you could love when you'd already shattered your chances with her?

When he turned the corner from Gordon Street onto Whitaker, he'd expected to see cars lined up on both sides of Whitaker and spilling onto the side streets, but there wasn't an excessive number of vehicles.

As he got closer to the inn, he recognized Charles's Cadillac, Ellie's white car and Daniel's truck parked near the Forsyth, among a handful of others that might have belonged to guests invited to the party. But he'd expected there to be more.

He stopped and pulled his phone from his pocket and glanced at the time, wondering if he was early. He wasn't. In fact, he was right on time. Maybe the others were late. Because the way Gigi had talked about the party when she'd announced it at the brunch he'd attended a couple of weeks ago, this was going to be a shindig. That was good, because it would allow him to wish the birthday girls well, have a drink with Jane where he could talk business, and then leave without it being obvious that he was cutting out early.

When he got into the lobby, he could see that the dining room was decorated with balloons and streamers and the table was set for a formal dinner.

A knot of people he didn't recognize was clustered at the side of the room. The next person he saw was Jane.

His heart stopped for the span of two beats.

And then she smiled at him.

"You're here," she said as she walked toward him. "I was afraid you wouldn't come."

"I wouldn't miss it." He suddenly realized he could breathe again. He remembered how she hadn't held a grudge and had made such an effort to put the past behind them when he'd first arrived in Savannah. She was that warm now, too. "Happy birthday."

She smiled at him, but her eyes looked sad. He wondered if he'd made a mistake coming tonight.

"Is this a dinner?" he asked, gesturing toward the table. "Or is it more of an open house?"

"It's a dinner. Just close friends and family."

"I didn't realize that," he said. "I'm honored to have been included."

He waited for her to smirk or scoff or do something to indicate the only reason he was there was that he was Charles's business partner, but she didn't. She led him into the dining room, where she took the flowers and champagne from him and set them on a small table that held other gifts.

Ellie hugged him hello and had just put a glass of wine into his hand when Gigi walked over.

"Liam, you handsome boy, you." She pulled him into a hug. "I'm so glad you could come and help this old lady and her granddaughter celebrate their birthdays. Charles tells me you just got back from New York today. Did you hire a new chef? Sounds like it was quite the emergency."

And just like that, Liam was swept back into the warm embrace of Jane's family. He didn't know what Jane had told them—if she'd told them anything about what had transpired in New York. If she hadn't, Gigi and Charles had surely sensed the tension at the awards ceremony. Sure, there'd been an emergency at La Bula, but he'd acted like a jackass. Still, they weren't reminding him of it. They weren't holding it against him. They were making him feel like family.

They were the family he'd always wanted.

Charles greeted him and was explaining that Gigi and the girls had self-catered the party—"They've been cooking all week. All we had to do was hire the servers. That's one of the perks of being a food family—" when he was pulled away and Liam finally found himself alone with Jane.

"How have you been?" Liam asked.

"Terrible," she said. "I owe you an apology for putting you on the spot like I did, Liam. I was just trying to help you connect with your dad because family is so important to me. I just... I'm sorry."

"It's okay," he said. "Actually, I called my dad a couple of days ago."

Jane gasped and her eyes brightened.

"Don't get too excited. This will be a slow process. We're going to have dinner when I'm there next month. So..." He shrugged. "We'll see."

"Will you keep me posted?"

Her words were a punch in the gut. She'd delivered them perfectly fine. Friend-to-friend. They felt like a handshake in lieu of a hug. Because her asking for him to *keep her posted* meant she didn't expect to be in the know, in his intimate inner circle where personal details were shared like a cup of sugar. But wasn't that the way he wanted it?

"Sure," he said. "And you know, we need to talk because I need you—er—I, uh… Wila needs you." He cleared his throat. "I need to know if you're still interested in preparing the desserts for Wila."

Her face went white a split second before she flushed.

He'd just said he needed her. Ugh. *Nice choice of words, idiot.*

But it was true. He needed her *help*. Help with desserts at Wila. And, in a different world, a different time and space and situation, he would've needed *her*. Her smart mouth, her stubborn streak, the way she could always make everything that was wrong feel right…

Her. He would've needed *her*.

His body and his heart tried to convince him that he did need *her*. But his brain reinforced the only way he could have her was if she supplied desserts to Wila.

"I need to… I, uh… Have you given any thought

to what we talked about in New York? Whether you want to do that?"

A few beats passed between them. Finally, she said, "You *need* me, huh?" The corners of her lips barely tilted up as she shook her head. "That arrangement might work, but we will need to set some ground rules. First, I'll need for you to cut me some slack. I'll be making *my* desserts now. You won't be my boss. So, if you're interested in what I have to offer, I think we can work out something. But that's the only way you can have me, Liam."

Thank God Charles called everyone to order by tapping his knife on his crystal wine goblet.

"May I have everyone's attention, please? Thank you for coming out to help me celebrate the women I love." He paused for effect and it worked.

People swooned. Liam couldn't keep from smiling because the guy was so obviously in love.

"Yes, it feels good to finally be able to say it out loud." He turned to Gigi and took her hand. "My darling, I love you. Why did we keep this happiness from ourselves for so long? Too long. But I guess the most important thing is that we're here now. We may be in our mideighties, but it doesn't lessen the love we feel for each other."

Gigi nodded and someone began pinging a crystal goblet and chanting, "Kiss! Kiss! Kiss! Kiss!" The others joined in. Charles and Gigi didn't disappoint them.

"Now, where was I?" Charles said. "You're getting me all hot and bothered, and I have something very important to do here."

He handed his glass to Daniel and took Gigi's hands in his. "My darling, I've lost track of how many years I've loved you. Shall we suffice to say that my love for you spans the ages and will last through eternity? Will you do me the great honor of being my wife?"

Charles reached into the breast pocket of his suit and pulled out a small blue box. Gigi's hands flew to her mouth as she nodded. He slid the large diamond into her finger.

As everyone rushed up to the happy couple to congratulate them, Liam's phone rang. He glanced at the number, intending to silence it, but when he saw the 718 area code—Brooklyn—something made him answer.

"Hello?" he said as he left the room, intending to take the call outside.

"Liam Wright?" asked a male voice. "This is Detective Walt Skenetti of the 84th Precinct of the New York City Police Department in Brooklyn. Is Malcom Wright your father?"

Liam's blood froze in his veins. "Yes. Why?"

"I regret to inform you that your dad has been shot in the line of duty."

Chapter Ten

After Liam booked himself on a red-eye flight to New York, he was stubbornly insisting on calling for a car to take him to the airport, but Jane put her foot down.

"At the risk of being a know-it-all, I think you're the one who's being unduly stubborn for not letting me take you to the airport. I'm right around the corner. If you let me take you, it would make me feel like I was doing something to help."

"If you put it that way…" he said.

As they pulled up to the passenger drop-off area at the airport, Liam said, "I'm sorry for being such a jerk in New York. I really am deeply sorry. Usually, when I treat people like that, they leave me. I'm glad you're still here."

Her breath caught, but she took a slow, deep breath and forced herself not to read more into it than it really was. She forced herself to be quiet and not fill the heavy silence. Jane could tell by looking at him that he wanted to say something.

"I've been doing a lot of thinking," he said. "Getting the call that my father could be dying and knowing that I might've just blown the last chance to make amends will do that."

His face was shadowed as he sat in the passenger seat, but she still saw his throat work as he swallowed.

"I guess I've been acting like I have all the time in the world..." He shrugged. "Like my business and the things I need to do are more important than..."

He sighed and shrugged. "I'm trying to tell you that you didn't deserve to be treated the way I treated you in New York. I was a total jackass. I guess I've been acting like a jackass for a while now and it seems like it's suddenly catching up with me...

"I'm not trying to make excuses, but all my life I felt like I was chasing a dream and everything was just outside of my grasp. When I won

America's Best Chef, things started falling into place, but every time something clicked, I felt like I had to work harder, run faster, not let any grass grow under me or I might lose it all. But since I got word about my dad, I've been thinking about what's important.

"It's not the life I've been chasing. It's the one I've been running away from. I've had a very clear vision of it and that that life includes you, Jane. But I wouldn't blame you if you didn't feel the same way. Hell, I wouldn't blame you if you were the one who turned around and ran the other way."

Jane wanted to say something, but the words were stuck in her throat. She wanted to reach out and hug him, but she was afraid if she did, her touch would break the spell and he would realize it was just the heightened emotions of the moment making him say these things. Once he got to New York and learned that his father was fine, he'd remember all the reasons she didn't fit into the life that he'd worked so hard to build from scratch and he'd push her away again.

He opened his car door and stepped out, got his suitcase out of the back seat. Jane still couldn't find any words that would make the situation right, but she managed to nod when he asked, "Can we talk about things when I get back from New York? Because I do need you, Jane. I need you."

The next morning, Jane checked her phone for about the hundredth time, hoping to see a text from Liam with an update on his father. The screen was persistently unchanged since the couple of exchanges they'd had after he'd arrived at Mount Sinai Hospital. The last she'd heard was that his father was in surgery and in critical condition.

It was touch and go.

Now, all Jane could do was wait and pray that his dad would pull through—and help out at Wila for as long as Liam needed to be away.

This morning, she and Charles were falling back into their old pre-Liam rhythm, but they were following Liam's newly established protocol. Things in the kitchen were exactly the same, but completely different than before Liam had come to Savannah.

It felt like something—or someone—was missing.

As the clock ticked toward 9:00 a.m., Charles, Jane and Joe Donoghue, Wila's sous chef, who had agreed to step up in Liam's absence, were the only ones in so far this morning. The rest of the kitchen staff wouldn't arrive for another hour. Jane was eager for the hustle and bustle to begin because the quiet gave her too much time to think.

Even as she prepared an army of mini mousse cakes—one of three offerings for the evening's dessert menu—she was having a hard time concentrating. The cakes were simple, a dome of chocolate hazelnut mousse nestled atop a brownie base and covered in a dark chocolate mirror glaze. It was a good thing she could prepare the recipe with her eyes shut, because her mind kept drifting to Liam and his father and what Liam had said to her at the airport after he'd gotten out of the car.

Can we talk about things when I get back from New York?

"Hey, darlin'." Gigi's voice startled Jane. She jumped and some of the mousse she was pouring into the mold sloshed onto the stainless-steel table. She turned around and saw her grandmother standing there clutching a small basket. "You looked far away. Any news from Liam?"

"Not yet. I keep checking." Jane nodded to her phone that she'd propped up against the wall at her station. "What do you have there?"

"It's Charles's breakfast. He loves my egg sandwiches. He had to be here so early. I thought I'd bring him some sustenance. You know how men are. Even if they work in the food industry, they'd starve their silly selves to death if they didn't have someone looking out for them."

Jane thought about the Russ & Daughters bagels Liam had gotten for her in New York. The guy had prided himself on being an island for so many years, he knew how to take care of himself. It had been a matter of self-preservation. He'd just started letting her in when he'd freaked out and closed the door.

"You love him," Gigi said. "Don't you?"

Jane blanched. She looked around to see if Joe was standing near enough to overhear Gigi, but she didn't see him.

"He loves you, too. I can tell. I don't know why you two nincompoops are fighting it, but don't wait until you're eighty-five years old. Don't waste the best years of your life when you could be enjoying them together."

She hadn't even told Gigi the full story, but somehow her grandmother knew. "Gigi—"

"Don't 'Gigi' me, honey. And don't wait for him to text you an update. Go to him. If the worst happens, he's going to need you there for support. If the best happens, and we're all praying everything will be okay, you two can talk things out. If the mountain won't come to Moses, then Moses must go to the mountain."

"I think it's Muhammad, not Moses, Gigi."

Gigi laughed. "Why do you always have to be right, you silly goose? Actually, in this case we're both wrong. It's Jane. Jane is the one who needs to go to the mountain. Because if you don't, you'll be making a mountain of a mistake."

Several hours after the surgery, Malcom Wright's condition had been updated from critical to stable. He would be moved from the intensive care unit to progressive care until the doctors were satisfied with his progress.

The attending doctor who'd looked in on him had said that Malcom's road to recovery would be long and challenging, but he was alive and they were optimistic that he would continue to improve.

Malcom had been conscious and alert enough to indicate that he was glad to see Liam, who had apologized to his father for the scene he'd caused when Jane had arranged the meeting.

"I thought she would've told you about the meeting," he'd said. "But don't hold it against her. I don't. The same way I don't hold your walking out against you. The only thing that would've made your mother happier than us mending our ways was to know that you'd found someone to share all your success. My gut tells me that this Jane is a keeper."

In the moment, Liam had noncommittally shrugged off his dad's assessment of Jane, turning the attention back on Malcom and telling him they'd talk about it later.

In reality, he hadn't known what to say to his dad about Jane. It was one thing to apologize to Jane for overreacting, it was another to talk to her to see if they could work things out. But what did that mean? Thinking of sharing his life with her was an altogether separate scary plane of its own. The thought set off all his internal alarms and sent his walls of self-protection flying up and locking in place.

What the hell was wrong with him?

Jane was the perfect woman for him. She understood him. She wasn't afraid to call him on his BS. In all the areas of his life, she made him want to be a better person.

But he was such a flawed person, he had so much baggage that he'd been dragging around his whole life, the thought of setting it down and letting someone love him—the thought of rendering himself vulnerable and opening himself up to getting hurt—made him want to run.

But what kind of life did you have if you didn't take chances?

As they prepared to move his dad to a different floor, Liam sat in the intensive care waiting room where the nurses had directed him and said they'd update him on where he could find his father. He'd texted Jane, but she hadn't replied. She'd asked him to keep her updated, but of course she would. She was that kind of person—kind, caring, hated to see someone suffering.

Her lack of response made him hesitate to text her again. He didn't want to bombard her with messages. He glanced at his watch. It was 3:00 p.m. This was a busy time at the restaurant as they prepared to open the doors at 5:00 p.m. She'd been gracious enough to step in at the restaurant, not only in her capacity as executive pastry chef, but also helping Charles oversee day-to-day operations of the kitchen while he was away.

Liam rubbed his eyes, trying to erase the fatigue. He was tired and hungry—but sleep and food would have to wait until after his father was settled.

So he sat there trying not to think about Jane, contemplating instead, how the timing of this emergency wasn't optimal.

But when did crisis ever take convenience into consideration?

He hadn't been willing to make time for his father when he'd been well. This was a wake-up call that was making him reevaluate everything that was important to him.

Jane is important.

Again, he looked at his phone to see if Jane had replied. She hadn't. He mentally shook off his disappointment as he clicked off his phone. He'd been given a second chance to make things right with his dad. While he wouldn't blame Jane for not wanting to give him a chance to make up for all his mistakes—hell, he had to call them what they were. Mistakes. He, who had such a low tolerance for mistakes and had a hard time giving others a second chance, seemed to need a lot of grace right now.

"Liam?"

In the split second before he looked up, the nurse's voice sounded exactly like Jane's. Then when he saw Jane standing in front of him, looking like an angel in cropped jeans and a white gauzy top, he stood. She closed the distance between them and the feel of her in his arms, the scent of jasmine and vanilla and cinnamon, canceled any doubt that he was wide awake. Holding her was balm for his soul.

"You're here," he said. "You came all this way?"

"I did." Her words sounded tentative. "I figured you probably hadn't eaten."

That's when he noticed the paper bag in her hand.

"I brought you something to eat. I thought you might be hungry."

"I'm starving."

She handed him the bag.

"I got your text when I got off the plane," she said. "I'm glad your father's doing well. Is everything still okay?"

"It is." Liam told her that they were moving him to progressive care and he was waiting to learn the details.

"That's such good news. I didn't reply because…" She shrugged. "Well, I wanted to answer you in person."

"Even better," he said.

"Really?" She drew in a breath and he realized she seemed nervous.

"Yes. Really."

"Oh, good. I was afraid that showing up might seem presumptuous. But, obviously, that didn't stop me." She lifted one shoulder and let it fall on an exhale. "I knew if I asked if you wanted me to come, you'd say no, but then I'd wonder if you really didn't want me here or if you were just being polite and not wanting me to make the trip. But I had to come. I figured you were looking out for your father, but I kept wondering who was taking care of you?"

He couldn't remember the last time anyone had cared whether he was okay. Not since his mom had died. Looking back, sure, his father had cared in his own way, but he'd been so broken over the loss, he'd kept Liam at arm's length.

Arm's length had become a way of life.

Liam couldn't remember the last time he'd let anyone close enough for them to care for him... like Jane cared.

But it was clear that Jane, in her stubborn persistence, wasn't going to let him push her away. Now, he needed to figure out exactly what he was going to do about it... About them.

After a day and a half in the progressive care unit, Malcom Wright was strong and stable enough to be moved to a regular room. With this news, Liam had decided he could finally leave the hospital and return to his own apartment for the first time since arriving back in New York after his father's accident.

Jane had been staying at the apartment for the two nights that she been in New York.

Liam had made it clear that he was happy she had come to New York, even after she'd asked him if it would be a bigger help to him if she went back to Savannah and worked with Charles. But when they had spoken with Charles, he had assured them that Jane's assistant, Tilly, was more than capable to hold down the pastry fort until Jane could return.

"It's more important that you be there for Liam and his father right now," Charles had said.

Jane had deferred to Liam, because even though she had taken it upon herself to come to New York, she'd wanted to make sure he was sure. He'd answered her with a deep kiss that left absolutely no doubt in her mind about how much he wanted her in New York.

As if that wasn't enough, he'd then suggested that they have dinner at La Bula.

"My dad wants me to stop hovering," Liam laughed. "How about if we grab a bite to eat at La Bula tonight?"

La Bula.

That was a big step.

She hadn't brought anything suitable to wear to dinner at Liam's restaurant.

"Let me treat you to something nice," he said. "I will see you at the restaurant for a late dinner. How about ten? I'm sorry it's so late, but that will be the best time for us to have dinner without any interruptions."

She had been so stunned that he wanted to have dinner at La Bula, she hadn't even had the presence of mind to realize he might have suggested the place because he needed to check in.

Still, it didn't escape her that he had asked her to join him. She'd given him the perfect out when she'd said she didn't have anything to wear. He could've suggested dinner at his place. He could've picked up something from the La Bula kitchen and brought it home with him.

But he didn't. He'd asked her to join him.

He'd even reserved a table for them.

The jumble of knots in her stomach cinched tighter. She couldn't help but think about what had transpired the last time she was at La Bula. The night he'd fired her in front of the entire kitchen staff. Sure, there would've been some turnover since she left, but the cornerstones of his kitchen were still in place. Maybe this was his way of making it up to her... Maybe this was his way of going public with their relationship. Because she couldn't imagine that he would kiss her the way he had in the hospital and sleep with her in his bed after taking her to his restaurant if this wasn't a relationship.

Of course, they hadn't talked about it at the hospital. She wasn't about to bring it up. His father's recovery and well-being had been the focus.

So now, as she stepped out of the car that Liam had hired to pick her up and bring her to La Bula, she took a deep breath and cleared her mind.

Tonight, she would walk in with her head held high, in her new black-lace Kate Spade dress and strappy black sandals. They would have a good meal and, even though she was nervous, going back to visit the dragon she hadn't been able to slay felt like the start to a whole new chapter in her life.

When she walked in, she saw a handful of guests lingering over wine and dessert. The maître d' was different from when she'd worked there, but she recognized some of the servers. A couple of them did a double take when they saw her. Then she saw Liam and he walked over and greeted her with a kiss. She might've looked to see the expressions on their faces, but she didn't care. Though, she had to admit, it would've been interesting to be a fly on the wall in the kitchen.

As if reading her mind, Liam said, "Do you mind if we take a quick run to the kitchen before we find our table? We close in a couple of hours. Things are starting to settle down." It felt like the knot in her stomach free-fell one hundred stories.

"Sure."

Might as well get that over with.

Then he surprised her by taking her hand.

The staff looked mostly unchanged, except for the pastry staff, of course. But Liam didn't make an issue of it. All he said was, "I know we're busy, but I wanted everyone to say hello to Jane Clark. For those of you who don't know Jane, she was our executive pastry chef before moving to Wila in Savannah."

Her former coworkers took time to say hello and congratulate her on winning the Oscar Hurd Foundation Award. Those she didn't know introduced themselves and extended their congratulations, too.

When things settled down, Jane realized that Liam had brought out several bottles of champagne. One of the servers was arranging at least a dozen champagne flutes on a stainless-steel table.

How sweet of him, Jane thought. *He's toasting my Oscar Hurd win.* This was his way of making up for what had happened between them the last time they were both in this kitchen.

She smiled at him and in that moment she thought she had never loved a man more than she loved him. He could be stubborn and cocky, and at times full of himself, but he was also gentle and caring and fiercely protective of those he loved.

Well, she was getting a little ahead of herself. Liam had never told her he loved her. Though, since she'd been with him in New York, she'd felt very loved. Standing here with him in the La Bula kitchen, she felt adored. With his history, saying the *L* word might take some time. But did they really have to label it?

If she was a betting woman—she laughed to herself—maybe he was right. Maybe she was a gambler at heart… Because she'd bet on him and on them for the win.

This felt like the start of something fabulous.

"Does everyone have a glass of champagne?" Liam asked. He waited for the last few people to get a flute. Then he took out his phone and began dialing a number.

"Are you there?" he said into the phone. "Can you hear me? Okay, good. You'll hook up the other call, right? Thanks. I'll wait."

What in the world was he doing? Jane didn't have time to ask or figure it out, because he acknowledged whoever was on the other end of the line and said, "I'm putting you on speaker."

Then he set the phone down and turned his attention to his staff.

"That's family on the phone. I wanted them to join us. They couldn't be here in person. So that's the next best thing."

What? Jane tried to ask, but her voice didn't make a sound.

"I hope you realize it," Liam said to the staff. "I consider each and every one of you family. That's why I couldn't think of a better place to do this than right here—surrounded by my family. As you all may or may not know, my personal family is very small—just my father and me—but I hope it's about to get bigger."

As Liam turned to Jane and reached for her hand, her heart hammered against her rib cage. Her body was very much awake, but she still wondered if she was dreaming.

"Jane, you have changed my life. We've had our

share of ups and downs, but isn't that what love is about? Experiencing ups and downs, and learning from the experiences, and becoming a better person because of it? Jane, with you, I have become a better man. You have taught me what love means. I love you and I am hoping that you will make me the happiest man in the world and be my wife. Jane Clark, will you marry me?"

Jane's breath caught.

Liam reached into the pocket of his sports coat and pulled out a small blue box. He flipped up the lid and something bright and lovely caught the light and winked at her as if it was a co-conspirator in Liam's surprise. Jane's hands flew up to her mouth.

"Yes! Oh, Liam, yes!"

A collective cheer went up in the kitchen and emanated from the phone.

As Liam put the ring, a brilliant, traditional round solitaire, on her finger, he said, "Our families are on the phone. Charles and Gigi are at Wila with the staff and they patched in my dad, who is recovering very nicely."

More happy noises sounded from the phone as Liam pulled her into his arms and kissed her so thoroughly that she knew she wasn't dreaming.

This was very real. Liam Wright was the man she'd been waiting for all her life and they were getting ready to live their very own dream come true.

* * * * *

Don't miss the last book in
The Savannah Sisters miniseries,
Her Savannah Surprise
available June 2020 from
Harlequin Special Edition.

And check out these other great
enemies-to-lovers romances:

The Best Intentions
by Michelle Major

Wyoming Special Delivery
by Melissa Senate

The Mayor's Secret Fortune
by Judy Duarte

Available now wherever Harlequin
Special Edition books and ebooks are sold!

*Officer Dante Santangelo doesn't "do" relationships,
but the busy single dad happily agrees to a secret
summer fling with younger free-spirited Gracie Bravo.
It's the perfect arrangement. Until Gracie realizes
she wants a life with Dante. Either she can say goodbye
at the end of the summer...or risk everything to
make this family happen.*

Read on for a sneak preview of
New York Times *bestselling author Christine Rimmer's
next book in the* Bravos of Valentine Bay *miniseries,*
Their Secret Summer Family.

"Gracie, will you look at me?"

Stifling a sigh, she turned her head to face him. Those
melty brown eyes were full of self-recrimination and
regret.

"I'm sorry," he said. "I never should have touched you.
I'm too old for you, and I'm not any kind of relationship
material, anyway. I don't know what got into me, but I
swear to you it's never going to happen again."

Hmm. How to respond?

Too bad there wasn't a large blunt object nearby. The
guy deserved a hard bop on the head. What was wrong
with him? No wonder it hadn't worked out with Marjorie.
The man didn't have a clue.

But never mind. Gracie held it together as he
apologized some more. She watched that beautiful mouth

move and pondered the mystery of how such a great guy could have his head so far up his own ass.

Maybe if she yanked him close and kissed him, he'd get over himself and admit that last night had been amazing, the two of them had off-the-charts chemistry and he didn't want to walk away from all that goodness, after all.

Yeah, kissing him might shut him up and get him back on track for more hot sexy times. It had worked more than once already.

But come on. She couldn't go jumping on him and smashing her mouth on his every time he started beating himself up for having a good time with her.

No. A girl had to have a little pride.

He thought last night was a mistake?

Fair enough. She'd actually let herself believe for a minute or two there that they had something good going on, that her long dry spell manwise might be over.

But never mind about that. Let him have it his way. She would agree with him.

And then she would show him exactly what he was missing. And then, when he couldn't take it anymore and begged her for another chance, she would say that they couldn't, that he was too old for her and it wouldn't be right.

Don't miss
Their Secret Summer Family *by Christine Rimmer,*
available May 2020 wherever
Harlequin Special Edition books and ebooks are sold.

Harlequin.com

Love Harlequin romance?

DISCOVER.

Be the first to find out about promotions, news and exclusive content!

 Facebook.com/HarlequinBooks

Twitter.com/HarlequinBooks

Instagram.com/HarlequinBooks

Pinterest.com/HarlequinBooks

ReaderService.com

EXPLORE.

Sign up for the Harlequin e-newsletter and download a free book from any series at **TryHarlequin.com**

CONNECT.

Join our Harlequin community to share your thoughts and connect with other romance readers!
Facebook.com/groups/HarlequinConnection

HSOCIAL2020

4451

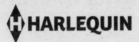

Heartfelt or suspenseful, inspiring or passionate, Harlequin has your happily-ever-after.

With new books published
every month, you are sure to find the
satisfying escape you know you deserve.

HNEWS2020